Main Course

The Upper East Side Cookbook

To Dusty,
    Caffè Taci, opera,
food, laughter, love
and <u>more</u> in 2012.
      Love you,
        Linda

PARSLEY PRESS   **LINDA OLLE**

January 14, 2012

THE UPPER EAST SIDE COOKBOOK:
Main Course

Volume two of a four-part series.

PARSLEY PRESS
New York, New York
2011

Parsley Press
New York, New York

Omnia vincit amor

Book Design by Bonnie Naugle.

Covers by Jane Freeman: Matisse (1993) and Catherine's Balcony
(1990).

Artwork by Catherine Stock, Joey Carolino, Phoebe Dingwall,
James De La Vega and Jennifer Olle.

Library of Congress catalogue data: 2011915412
ISBN-13: 978-1466268944
ISBN-10: 1466268948

"If I knew you were coming I'd have baked a cake, baked a cake, baked a cake." Eileen Barton

"Let me sleep all night in your soul kitchen,
Warm my mind near your gentle stove."
Jim Morrison

"Remind me to tell you about the time I looked into the heart of an artichoke." Bette Davis in *All About Eve*

"Will you serve the nuts? I mean, will you serve the guests the nuts?" Myrna Loy in *The Thin Man*

INTRODUCTION

*I*n late 2008, I took on the task of feeding a noisy and talkative parrot next door while its owner, my glamorous neighbor, Parsley Cresswell, accustomed herself to the big house. She won the cell decoration contest at Christmas, no surprise to anyone who knows Parsley and her holiday flare.

It wasn't what she did or did not do that kept her there so much as whom she knew. She'd have been out on bail were it not for her associations with a certain hedge fund pioneer being investigated by the S.E.C. The D.A. put pressure on her to turn state's evidence. This is something she would never do, if it meant betraying a friend, even a late friend—who died while she happened to be with him.

I knew she wasn't guilty, as I said at my deposition. I, a C.P.A., gave a careful accounting of Parsley's trustworthiness as a neighbor, her winning ways as a stylist, and the recipe for her signature onion pie. I said I expected there was no case whatsoever, and that Ms. Cresswell should be released to come home immediately! And, I'd still say that, even knowing her much better now.

*W*hile Parsley Cresswell was away, I used my forensic accounting skills in this work of excavation. You can find a time capsule of the late 20th Century in her cookbook diary.

We met in 2002, when I rented the studio apartment next to hers in a crumbling brownstone. PC, my new arbiter of style, swanned around Seventh Avenue, dressed to the nines, and sat along runways, taking notes. I wore businesslike skirts, Oxford shirts, and pumps, and occupied a cubicle on Wall Street where I crunched numbers. (At Parsley's suggestion, I started decorating my workspace with a fresh bunch of flowers every Monday. What an improvement!) Some nights I came home late from work to people in the hallway with wine glasses and cigarettes (cough, cough), from a party. Other times, the heady cooking smells put me in a state of perpetual hunger, like I lived next to a four-star restaurant where I could never afford to eat.

Parsley dropped off first-rate leftovers of mushroom tarts, Chicken Wellington, and an egg-y chocolate cake (which turned out to be from a mix, she openly admitted).

Everything she cooked was healthy and sensuous. I got to know her not over dinner so much as from her files —recipes and menus, and receipted expenditures from such stores as Bonwit Teller and Gotham Book Mart; restaurants Café des Artistes and Tavern on the Green; and a pre-Fairway food emporium, Petak's. She kept the receipts of everything she ever bought—a treasure trove for a bookkeeper.

I considered her cool even before I knew about the long ago weekends she spent with the one she refers to in her diary as "Bobby." She always turned up the music and sang at the top of her lungs while she cooked. She has been heard by her neighbors to sing in Spanish while cooking, also French ("La Vie en Rose" and "Toréador") Italian ("Quando m'en vo" and "O mio babbino caro"), and Portuguese ("Mas Que Nada"). Her top ten kitchen platters included Carole King and Joni Mitchell, Barry Manilow, Barry White, Prince, and Bob Dylan—though never Joan Baez, whom she practically considered a rival, mysteriously enough.

If anything revives the hippie ethos it's Parsley as a college student saving up orange peels, stirring a vat of marmalade on the stove, and soaking three pounds of beans to feed her commune. The style of thrift ensured that through the wild disco years and beyond Parsley remained a committed puritan, because she could afford to be no wilder than that.

Parsley collected recipes from beaux du jour. "I'm a

sucker for any man with a recipe up his sleeve," she'd said over Earl Grey tea and maple walnut scones one teatime. She had many loves. Did she date too much? I consider her male positive rather than man crazy.

She kept harissa, sriracha, Tabasco sauce, black and multi-colored pepper corns in grinders at hand for guests. Various friends found Parsley's cooking a little on the bland side. It must be said that her Japanese boyfriend found the blandness "just right." He especially admired her hand with tofu.

The sous chef from Chanterelle taught her quiche à la fromage. "Not to mention, all of the basic sauces," she pointed out. From him she learned to chiffonade basil (crush leaves together and slice with a sharp knife into ribbons), and he brought dinner home sculpted into a Reynolds Wrap swan. When he returned to Nice he left her his parrot, Gougère.

"His father had a *légion d'honneur*," she mentioned, using her typically exaggerated pronunciation of any foreign language. She told me she learned how to make Pets de Monja in the kitchen of a matador in Seville, along with the Mexican song "La Bamba."

The Japanese boyfriend and the West African boyfriend each contributed their national styles of cuisine. The Japanese fellow was a big drinker and the African totally abstained. Parsley's own attitude to drinking was moderate, but following her golden rule, Quum Romae fueris. "When in Rome, do as the Romans," she abstained when her partner did.

Her food diary includes photos of table settings with spare ikebana arrangements and lavish floral centerpieces with pheasant feathers. She took photos of meals she cooked alongside the New York Society library book that she was reading with dinner. One picture featured a love letter beside a dessert plate and her customary glass of ice water. It wasn't merely thrift. "Thoreau's drink was water," she confided to her journal gastronomique. Practically indifferent to wine, though knowledgeable about cru levels, she wrote, "My favorite cocktail is the shrimp cocktail."

Parsley worked in the fashion world and has always loved accessories—props like a riding crop and a 19th Century equestrian top hat. Her storied walk-in closet was full of hats, barely worn couture pieces, fur and gloves. There was a corset that laced up the back and an Edwardian ruff for her long neck. In fact, she was wearing the lace ruff and corset when she was arrested and taken to Rikers Island, for her formal portrait, facing the camera and in profile. It must be said that Parsley's so-called mug shots are among the most beautiful I have seen. Anyone would be proud of them. She was clear-eyed, in full make-up, with excellent straight posture, and neither drunk nor ill-tempered. She was Garbo-esque.

In the Eighties and Nineties Parsley ate very well, took notes, and was known to bribe a waiter for a recipe from a top chef. She began to use more upscale ingredients after her move to the posh Upper East Side, where there are more restaurants than grocery stores, where people eat very well though seldom cook. The book you are reading spans Parsley's twenties, thirties, and forties—and beyond. (These recipes were in her repertory long before the one-year timeframe, 2008, of *The Upper East Side Cookbook: Setting the Table in a Time of Slender Means*.)

In PC's fussiest cooking stage, she created a smoked salmon cake of a clock face, with chives at midnight, salmon caviar and dill to serve an international cast of New Year's guests on the eve of Y2K. When she partied among people from every continent she felt "at my happiest ever! And there are so many exotic recipes to collect," she wrote in her journal.

In the projected Volume III of *The Upper East Side Cookbook*, Parsley is revealed to pare down her lifestyle further, much further—and to teach her fellow inmates to keep valuable food diaries, transcribing recipes from the most memorable occasions of their lives.

Don't wait for an engraved invitation, let's enjoy Parsley in the 20th Century. *Bon appétit* and welcome to the Upper East Side. Parsley's best dishes, as well as her tips for living, are tasty, bite-size, and low-cal.

Fran E. Smith C.P.A.

New York, New York
May 1, 2009

*P*arsley's exact age might be impossible to pin down, however we know she is old enough to remember the Cuban Missile crisis. She spent her childhood on a farm in the Midwest, in a farmhouse with her parents and grandparents, and played in a fallout shelter with her sister and girl cousins, with Barbie dolls dressed in miniature haute couture. They and their mothers wore mother-daughter matching A-line dresses. Parsley dressed her Barbie as Mrs. Robinson, in leopard coat and tall black mules.

Her family visited Aunt Pistachio in New York, and they saw the United Nations. In the UN gift shop young Parsley chose a hardcover book on holidays and recipes from around the world. She focused on Shrove Tuesday crêpes from France. The crêpe pancake was a morning feat that Parsley strove to perfect. In junior high she left the crêpe behind to perform the fluffy omelet. Parsley will still make you an omelet at the drop of a hat. A fixation with the perfect grilled cheeseburger came in her high school years.

Parsley's mother, Courgette, preferred when people

cooked for her, and tried to instill in her children the idea
that "It doesn't taste as good when you make it yourself."
Her daughters never understood this expression. Parsley
and her sister, Frito Kahlo Cresswell, felt their own cooking
was way superior to that of others. Their party trick was
English Muffin Pizzas, with commercial pizza sauce,
crumbled Italian sausage with fennel seed, and shredded
mozzarella, baked in a hot oven for ten minutes. When
Parsley grew up, she developed a more mature version of
the beloved English muffin pizza.

Puff-Pastry Pizzas

Caramelize a chopped Spanish onion and green pepper.
Add tomato sauce to the pan. Roll out puff pastry on a
surface dusted with cornmeal. Cut circles with a glass.
With a spoon, add a smear of onion sauce. Stack: 2 basil
leaves, tomato slice, black olives, anchovy (optional), Parmesan, a drizzle of olive oil, and red pepper flakes. Bake
at 350°F, 15 minutes, until the pastry on the edges turns
golden brown around the edges. Shower with basil leaves
before serving.

$\mathcal{B}$oth of Parsley's parents had jobs; meals were prepared by Grandma Kolache, a famous cook, who lived with her husband on the first floor. Kolache's grandmother came over on a ship from Bohemia, a former kingdom in the Czech Republic, with her life savings sewn between the ruffles of her petticoat. The food Parsley grew up on had an Eastern European slant, cooked in two kitchens, the main one and the unheated back kitchen, which had a midden (a container

DRAWING BY PHOEBE DINGWALL

for scraps to be taken to the barnyard animals). All of the ingredients were produced on the farm.

Minty Parsley Cresswell, Kolache's brother in Milwaukee, frequently visited the farm, and the red carpet was rolled out for him. He arrived in a Lincoln Town Car driven by a chauffeur who was a former jockey. Uncle Minty weighed over 400 lbs and was always well dressed, in a bespoke suit with matching shoes, topcoat and hat. He introduced Parsley's family to smoked salmon, jumbo shrimp, soul music, and the schottische. He was light on his feet when he danced.

Married to Aunt Rose, Minty was her second husband. Rose was the only one in Parsley's family who'd been divorced, and it gave her a certain renown. Rose was often too busy to visit Minty's family on the farm, so the family had Minty all to themselves. The meat recipes that Parsley collected include Uncle Minty's Salty Chocolate Fudge, made with beef lard, a recipe transcribed by his secretary on an Underwood typewriter.

Kolache cooked up a storm whenever she had a feeling that her brother was due. She claimed to communicate telepathically with Minty. No need for a telephone call— they had the Bohemian gypsy skill of being able to divine what the other was thinking or planning, over a distance of thirty miles—a useful skill to have before text messaging was available.

Rarely was she wrong, and the table was set for two more, and much more food was prepared, when Uncle

Minty and his chauffeur arrived on the long, gravel drive-way. When Kolache was mistaken about his visit, they had leftovers for pot pies.

Chicken Pot Pie

Commercial short crust or puff pastry
2 T butter
1 T olive oil
1 cup chopped leeks and onions
2 large carrots, peeled and cubed
3 ribs celery, peeled and sliced
1 T sage or tarragon, chopped
1 T thyme leaves
1 or 2 juicy lemons
1 cup heavy cream
1 cup leftover peas (or frozen peas, defrosted)
2 cups cooked chicken, shredded or cubed
Leftover sweet corn, 1 or 2 ears, sliced from the cob

Remove pastry from the freezer and place in the refrigerator overnight. Sauté onions and leeks, carrots and celery, in butter and olive oil. Add chopped herbs, lemon zest and lemon juice, and cream. Allow to thicken, stirring occasionally, on the stove.

Arrange peas, cooked chicken, and corn in a Pyrex dish. Pour in the cream and vegetables, and gently combine.

Roll out on a floured surface the refrigerated pastry, and cut to more than cover the pie (use a top layer only). After transferring pastry to the filled dish, cut a pattern for the heat to escape. Brush crust with an egg wash. Bake at 400°F for about 30 minutes, or until the crust is golden and cooked through.

*W*hen Parsley required eyeglasses at school, her mother said, "You look fine in glasses. You look *even better* in glasses."

Thus began PC's love affair with accessories. When it came to hats, gloves, jewelry and scarves, too much was never enough. On Halloween, in recent years, our Parsley has been a witch, a goth, a dominatrix, and a goth witch dominatrix. Even in costume, she wears comfortable shoes. When prominent socialite Bran Kempner, wearing Galliano high heels, slipped and broke her hip, Parsley said, "That's it!" to uncomfortable footwear.

As much as she admires edgy fashion, her favorite era and look is embodied in Elaine Benes on "Seinfeld"—so comfortable, so proper, in tailored jacket and flowy long skirt or trousers, pumps, fluffy hair.

Back then, everyone wore comfortable shoes and wouldn't dream of wearing anything else! Parsley and her friend Fig Tornatore figured out that *the* most comfortable shoes on the planet were made by the Italian company Famolare. They went through two pairs apiece of the wavy soled Famolares, in black and in brown. Parsley regularly looks to eBay to check if there are any more, of any color, still out there.

Inspired by Fig, who always dresses up, Parsley marks All Hallows Eve by wearing her well-detailed, perfectly fitted costume to work. Parsley had a job out of college at a women's magazine, and later graduated to a women's fashion magazine. Most days her outfits were slightly out-landish—her office wear included hemlines mini to maxi. On Halloween she was, of course, more dramatic, going to work got up as Morticia Addams. (It must be said that some people didn't notice that Parsley was in costume.)

To create the right eerie atmosphere for the tricker-or-treaters, Parsley played *Fantastic Symphony* by Berlioz and Strauss's *Salome*, and she made blondies and brownies with fresh mint gathered from her terrace garden before the first frost. She handed them out wrapped in scary little poems by Emily Dickinson.

She stood in the doorway of her ten-apartment brown-stone, in a Marie Antoinette wig with a ship in full sail and a floor-length gown with a bustle on either hip, pre-tending to be the lady of the house and greeting trick-or-treaters. Not eating even one mint brownie herself, when two batches of brownies were given away, she finished the evening feeling oddly satisfied. She dipped into Robert Burns's epic *Tam o' Shanter* five minutes before she drifted off to sleep. True to her fashion-conscious roots, she cut straight to the part about Cutty Sark (a character named for her fashion-forward cut-off skirt).

One Halloween she made the terrible mistake of passing out ice-cream sandwiches. A neighbor mother complained that it would stain her child's rented costume, refused to let her have one, and led the youngster away in tears. Their Chihuahua was dressed as a witch. "To die for," Parsley wrote. "Gorgeous rich kids in their awesome costumes. Though Halloween on Carnegie Hill has its Diane Arbus moments—sullen devils and indifferently dressed ghosts."

Parsley felt that insofar as baking was gluten-free, it was guilt-free. When she served gluten-free brownies and blondies as a dinner party dessert, she made them into ice-cream sandwiches, using vanilla for the mint brownies and chocolate ice cream for the mint blondies.

Gluten-Free Mint Brownies and Blondies

Add to one health-food-store purchased, non-gluten brownie or blondie mix, ½ tsp peppermint essence or coconut essence, and ½ cup chopped mint leaves, mashed with 1 T butter. Bake according to directions on the box. Decorate with plastic black widow spider rings.

*I*sn't the UES a little boring? a hip, downtown friend wagered. "Not at all," said Parsley, quick to defend her turf. "After all, Lady Gaga attended school on the Upper East Side!" Lady Gaga went to Sacred Heart.

Parsley went to a Roman Catholic grade school. It was the convent's equivalent of a restaurant experience for a lady parishioner, such as her mother, Courgette, a good cook, to deliver a potluck dinner to the sisters. They signed up seven mothers each week to bring them home-cooked dinners, with the explanation that cooking for the convent would free up the sisters to have more time for good works. "A likely story," said Filbert, Parsley's dad.

Parsley remembers that Courgette prepared for this lazy order of nuns a paprika chicken noodle dish, sprinkled with poppy seed, and a string-bean side dish made with Campbell's mushroom soup and topped with French's French Fried Onions. The beans, especially, were a hit at the convent. One beautiful nun said the meal was the best she ever had.

"Does your family always eat this well?" said the sister

named for the martyred Saint Velveeta, who was burned (some say "melted") at the stake in Florence along with Savonarola. "I'll bet she says that to all the Altar Society gals," said Filbert, with a wink.

Parsley had always liked nuns' habits. Sister Velveeta told Parsley that her order's habit was designed by the Paris House of Worth. PC, in the seventh grade, recounted it in her early diary. Velveeta taught English and demystified sentence structure by charting it on the bulletin board. "I want you all to love words and keep diaries," she said, meaningfully.

"People generally like *Breakfast at Tiffany's* the most, but my favorite Audrey Hepburn movie, now and forever, is *The Nun's Story*," Parsley said.

*P*arsley was politicized at college and took part in demonstrations. She was an "A" student, although she had an imperfect education and felt a sense of uncertainty regarding the classics, world wars, monarchies, and Greek mythology. She knew that living on the Upper East Side was like the Sword of Damocles or Occam's razor, but she couldn't remember which.

She carried her lunch to school and ate it, discreetly, during class so she could swim over the lunch hour. She hid her chewing behind a book. "Stealth food to eat in class or take to the library must be silent," Parsley wrote, with a fountain pen with purple ink. "It can't be nuts or crunchy—even some whole wheat breads are ruled out. Must be silent. Must not give off a delicious smell and make neighbors jealous."

An alluring stealth food Parsley carried was the **Curried Egg-Tuna Salad** sandwich—though it could almost be eliminated because of its too delectable smell. Make regular old tuna salad with mayonnaise and chopped onion, carrot, and celery. Add one hard-boiled egg, crumbled, and 1 tsp curry powder. "The adventurous will add a handful of raisins and cashews," was the marginalia of this recipe.

A classmate from India taught her how to crisp papadums in the microwave and how to make this economical and delicious lentil and rice dish with caramelized onions. Another classmate served the dorm kitchen classic, cauliflower with caramelized onions. "When you learn to cook for yourself it is essential to learn how to caramelize an onion," she wrote in her early food diary.

Mujhaddara (Lentils and Caramelized Onions)

2 Spanish onions
2 cups lentils
1 cup basmati rice
½ cup olive or vegetable oil
5 cups water or vegetable stock
Pinch of cinnamon
1 T cumin
2 T dal masala or garam masala (Indian spice blend)
Cayenne pepper
Salt

Cut up one onion into thin slices. Chop the other. Cook the sliced onion in oil until practically crisp, in the heavy soup pot you will be using to cook the lentils. Put caramelized onions aside.

Sauté the chopped onion. Add lentils and seasoning.

Add water, bring to a boil, and simmer on medium for twenty minutes, until the lentils become tender. Add the rice and cook half an hour more. Before removing from the stove, check that the rice has fully cooked, and if not, cook for longer, adding a little boiling water if more is needed. Serve topped with caramelized onions, chopped parsley and cilantro. Serve olives and pickles, harissa and red pepper flakes, on the side.

Cauliflower with Caramelized Onions

Cut out the core and steam a whole cauliflower in salted boiling water for ten minutes or until cooked. Slice one or two large onions thinly, and fry at medium in butter and a dab of olive oil (to keep the butter from burning). Drain cauliflower and place on a dish. Spoon caramelized onions over the top and serve. Variations: crumbled tortilla chips and grated cheddar.

ILLUSTRATION BY PHOEBE DINGWALL

*P*arsley and her mother, Courgette, took a trip to Holland. In Amsterdam, they tried the fabled Space Cake and were not much impressed with how it tasted, and frankly disappointed with the salubrious effects they'd heard so much about. They followed it up with a walk through the Vondelpark and more museum-going. Then, the effects of the Space Cake kicked in, and they had the best ever visit to an art museum anywhere, to the Van Gogh museum, oohing and ahhing over the portraits and his sunflowers, his irises, and his pink roses.

The next day they found themselves at the nude beach in The Hague. Mom took a photo with her Instamatic of her daughter sunbathing in just her bikini bottoms. Parsley wrote in her diary, *"Whereas I was only topless, and so many around us were totally nude, I felt practically overdressed."* Her mother wore a one-piece, red-white-and-blue Jantzen.

"A donkey and cart was led down the beach selling delicious boiled shrimp on a bed of ice and Heinekens. The perfect meal." They enjoyed Indonesian Gado-Gado, a peanut sauce served with steamed and blanched vegetables, on a cruise around Amsterdam's canals by night.

Gado-Gado Sauce

½ cup vegetable oil
1⅓ cup fresh ground peanut butter
3 cloves garlic minced
1 shallot or small onion, chopped
2 drops oyster or fish sauce
½ tsp sugar
½ tsp cayenne
1 T soy sauce
2 cups water
Salt
Juice of one lemon
Fresh mint or basil for garnish

Simmer all but the lemon juice on the stove for ten minutes. Cool, then blend, adding lemon juice. Taste and adjust with salt. Garnish with fresh mint or basil.

Serve with an artistic assortment of raw and blanched vegetables, including sweet corn, beans and sugar snap peas, cucumbers, bean sprouts, and boiled new potatoes. For meat eaters, add a couple of boiled chicken breasts, deboned and shredded.

*S*he woke with a naked Scotsman in her bed. His Black Watch kilt lay on the floor. Their mutual ardor for poet Robert Burns brought them together. The night before, they'd met at a Burns supper, which had gotten out of hand, as all Burns suppers are meant to.

On Robert Burns's birthday, January 25, she held a formal banquet with poetry, a bagpiper, and Scottish country dancing to a fiddler. Her Burns supper was attended by no less than four men in kilts of different tartans, with poetry recitation, singing and rolling up the rug and dancing to a fiddler. She prepared the traditional menu, Burns's favorite meal: Mashed potatoes ("tatties") and puréed turnips ("neeps"), accompanied by a haggis sausage in a sheep's stomach casing—or an alternate meat loaf, more easily assembled. Scotch whisky is de rigueur, at least for the toast to "Rabbie" Burns. Ideally the haggis is "piped in" or brought to the table with a bagpipe serenade. A toast to the ladies and a toast to the gents are followed by a reading of each guest's favorite Burns poem. She loves the sweet poems *To a Mouse* and *To a Louse*. Her favorite lines are: "O, wad some Power the giftie gie us / To see oursels as others see us!"

Her favorite national costume is the kilt. Her favorite Alexander McQueen season is the Widows of Culloden.

This is her version of haggis and the Burns supper.

Haggis Meat Loaf

Olive oil
1 onion, diced
3 cloves garlic, minced
½ calf's liver or chicken livers
1 egg
¼ cup pistachios, roasted in frying pan
1 tomato, diced
1 lb. ground lamb
½ cup stock or wine
Salt and black pepper
½ tsp cayenne
½ tsp nutmeg, freshly ground
¼ tsp ground cloves
¼ tsp ground ginger
1 lemon, juice and zest
⅓ cup chopped parsley
1 cup old-fashioned rolled oats
breadcrumbs

Preheat oven to 400°F. Sauté onion and garlic in olive oil. Purée liver (or chop with a knife), add to a bowl and mix in with your hands the other ingredients, apart from the breadcrumbs. Add a bit of milk if it seems to need moisture. Transfer to a loaf pan and shape for meatloaf. Sprinkle breadcrumbs on top. Cover with a piece of foil and bake for 50 minutes or until done. Let rest, unmold to a serving platter, and cut, reciting Rabbie Burns' poem, *To a Haggis* (optional). Serve with potatoes and turnips (tatties and neeps).

Tatties (Potatoes) Peel and cube potatoes. If you are using organic potatoes, peel and leave some of the potato skin on. Cover with salted water and bring to a boil, cook twenty minutes or until tender to the fork. Mash and whip in milk and butter. Salt and pepper. (Alternately, boil tiny red potatoes in salted water for 20 minutes or until soft, tested with a fork. Do not over-boil. Serve with butter, salt, and chopped parsley.)

Neeps (Turnips) Peel a few turnips, a parsnip and carrot. Boil until tender, and mash with butter. Salt and pepper. Garnish with thyme or parsley.

With the dawn of 1984, Parsley recalled her student crush on writer Eric Arthur Blair, a.k.a. George Orwell, who went into mines and reported on the conditions of coal miners, and whose compassion for his fellow man was clear in all he wrote. Parsley said of Orwell, "I have only to gaze on the few black-and-white photographs of him to lower my blood pressure!"

A reporter asked Orwell to choose the quality he would most like to have, and he said that he would like to be "irresistible to women." He asked one after another to marry him and they turned him down. Parsley can't imagine how anyone could say no to Eric Arthur Blair! He identified so closely with people who were hard up that he could never again criticize the lack of energy in a person who is out of work. He wrote that he couldn't really "enjoy a meal at a smart restaurant."

She said she thought he might not feel comfortable on the Upper East Side, and "I wonder what Eric would have made of the current problems the world is experiencing."

Parsley likes her tea as Orwell did: on the strong side,

sugarless, with a cloud of milk, and in a mug rather than a teacup and saucer. Loose tea in a pot instead of teabags. Afternoon tea is often her happiest time of the day, even on Rikers Island. Indeed, she said she popularized it among her fellow inmates.

Maple Walnut Scones

½ cup unsalted butter
½ cup walnuts or pecans
1½ cups flour
½ cup sugar
¼ tsp baking powder
¼ tsp baking soda
¼ tsp salt
½ cup heavy cream
1 T and 1 tsp maple syrup
1 egg
1 additional egg for glaze
1 T cream

Leave the butter out overnight so it softens. Preheat oven to 400°F and toast walnuts or pecans for 5 minutes. Cool and chop. In a large bowl, whisk flour, sugar, baking powder and baking soda and salt. Add softened butter and with your fingers, blend it in. Stir in chopped nuts. In a small bowl, blend cream and maple syrup. Beat egg and milk in a separate bowl, reserving 1 tablespoon of the mixture in a separate bowl for glaze. Add the egg mixture and do not over-mix the dough.

Place lumps on a parchment-paper lined cookie sheet.
Blend egg and cream and brush glaze on top of scones.
Bake for twenty minutes or longer, till golden brown.

*T*wo size-zero neighbors in red-soled heels, standing at the corner of Fifth Avenue with their standard poodles, greeted one another. "You look great! You haven't gained an ounce!" said one. "Thanks, it must be all the stress," said the other.

Parsley rolled her eyes. "They went to the School of Soft Knocks."

Children here are not spoiled and whiny, as one would expect, but overall, well mannered and quiet. "They have a great support system of tutors, shrinks, and antidepressants," Parsley explained.

"People are so different here that we might as well secede from New York City and form our own principality, like the Vatican or Washington D.C.," she said.

The Upper East Side was the planet of agelessness, so we had a chance to see this as the norm. "As George Orwell said, 'At fifty, everyone has the face he deserves.' I used to think that hair color and makeup were deception. Now I think they're magic."

Parsley said facelifts only make people look older. "My brainy friends in the publishing world aren't the ones getting botoxed or having their lips inflated. There's more of an aging naturally, with moral indignation, among them." Whereas she looked forward to growing old.

"Oh yes, when the time comes, I have every intention of shaving my head and going gray dramatically!"

"When would that be?" I ventured.

"The day before my seventieth birthday," answered Parsley. "Um, or the day just after!"

No event could make her wear uncomfortable footwear. Always prepared, she never left home without MILK: acronym for money, ID, lipstick, keys. Advised by her Aunt Pistachio, a flight attendant for TWA, she packed light, preferably just one carry-on bag. (Checked luggage might go astray.) She packed essentials, never forgetting to bring a small notebook to transcribe a recipe. Later, the size of the handbag grew to accommodate a mobile phone, spare pair of socks, and the reusable Rubbermaid container for restaurant fare (Parsley was green ahead of her time), and corkscrew.

She reviewed her recipe file to find meals of a complicated nature, though for herself she cooked the simplest fare (sautéed spinach with shaved parmesan, as a main course). She saw the irony and ditched a lot of fancy recipes, and saved a great many, especially when the dish approached a home run.

With an expensive pair of birding binoculars around her neck, a gift from a swain, Parsley foraged in Central Park for mushrooms sprouting high up on a tree trunk. She would stealthily cull a choir of oyster mushrooms, depending upon whether they are "absolutely fresh, fresh, fresh" (grown the very night before) and if there was no one around to see her do it. She placed her treasure in tissue paper and a recycled orange-and-white Zabars bag, then dined alone on her "home run," **Oyster Mushrooms** sautéed with garlic and onion and served on Tom Cat toast, with baby lettuces, chopped fresh herbs, fresh ground pepper, and a pinch of coarse sea salt.

The "home run" was born around the time that she was writing for the haute cuisine quarterly, *Yummy*. "It could be the couscous with roasted vegetables and grated Parmesan that your boyfriend cooked for you on a rainy afternoon. It makes your cheeks flush and your eyes well up. The taste of it renews hope. A **Home Run** is any cooking that sets off a wave of nostalgia. Like your grandmother's recipe, in her handwriting, it's powerful stuff. It was the dinner that left you feeling satisfied, that warmed you on a cold day. It was just what you craved, and you took notes, so you'll have it again whenever you want. Thick soup made from boiled carrots, turnip and parsnips, blended with stock, and garnished with yogurt, a sprig of mint, and red pepper flakes….

"Served on fine linen by candlelight in your best soup

bowl, it's a work of art. One night it's salad and rice, and **Blackened Swordfish**, in 2 tablespoons Louisiana Creole seasoning, fried in oil in cast iron on high heat. A home run with all the bases loaded might be your wine-poached pear with olive oil, rock salt and pepper, with raisin bread, dolce Gorgonzola, and a crisp Albariño on the side. Afternoon tea with *pain perdu* (French toast) dusted with confectioners' sugar and green-tea ice cream served in a teacup."

Parsley related, "As my close personal friends, Mick and Keith, used to say, 'You can't always get what you want, but if you try sometimes, you might find, you get what you need'."

Often she jotted down the home run's components and filed it beside an Instamatic photo—as the fashion designers would use—of that meal, posed attractively with an embroidered cloth napkin, besides the front page of *The Daily News* or the library book she was reading. She recorded an impressionistic vision of where and when this was cooked. Sometimes she sketched and colored it in with eye shadows from her makeup kit.

"One night, your body screams out for a Green Pie, easily accomplished. If you have the time to shop, substitute fresh chard (veins removed) for the spinach. If you don't want to fire up the oven and bake it, you can do a scrambled version on top of the stove: home run with all bases loaded."

Green Pie

1 10 oz. package frozen leaf spinach (or fresh)
1 onion, diced
3 cloves garlic, chopped
1 leftover baked potato, skin removed
Fresh sage or tarragon, thyme
Parsley, chopped
1 pinch of red pepper flakes
1 pinch freshly ground nutmeg
1 pinch cinnamon
1 egg
½ cup Jarlsberg, cheddar, or Parmesan, grated
½ cup seasoned breadcrumbs or sliced almonds

Remove spinach from the freezer and defrost. Fry onion and garlic in oil. Add diced potato, drained spinach, seasoning and egg, and top with cheese. Heat a frying pan and roast breadcrumbs or almonds, until toasted. Sprinkle on top. Bake twenty minutes in a 375°F oven.

(Volume 1 of *The Upper East Side Cookbook* contains an alternate version, Crustless Green Pie, using a cup of Wisconsin cheddar cheese and using fresh chard and zucchini instead of frozen spinach.)

*B*etween Memorial Day and Labor Day, the neighbors are at a shoreline dining on seafood. Children are neither seen nor heard. You can ride your bike down the middle of the avenue with no traffic and you have the Upper East Side to yourself. Why go anywhere?

On the Tuesday after Labor Day I saw Parsley waltz down the stairs. She loved her vacation and returned to work and her workmates with the happy hope of a student beginning a new term. Pearls set off a tan. Her tidy coif, her belted, fringed white dress, her kitten-heel pumps—she was *Elegante, por detrás y por delante.* (She'd said, "The matador taught me that expression.")

It must be said that Parsley could not be described as looking "hot." It was never her intention to look like a fox—she was her own species. She favors high necklines and she does not feel constrained to smile and show her teeth. Parsley grins. Parsley winks.

"Told them I was in the Costa del Sol. I was really on the Costa del New Jersey." She gave a conspiratorial wink. "Can there be any nicer shore than the Jersey shore? I doubt it! I had a super time."

Next I saw her when I returned late after completing a Q4 tax filing. "If the company claims to be worth that much, then it has a bigger tax burden," I explained to my supervisor. "Whatever!" she replied.

Parsley looked chic whatever she was doing, and that night I found her standing in a dumpster on Madison Avenue, in what looked to me like a ball gown but what may have been her office wear. She was barefoot, with sandals buckled together and slung over one shoulder. As I got closer I could see she was culling discarded lobby bouquets.

Gracefully she hopped down from the dumpster and removed a pair of rubber flip-flops from her handbag and slipped them on. If Parsley was taken aback to find me watching her climb through a dumpster, she recovered her dignity in a flash. "Isn't it a good idea to carry flip-flops? Do you do this too, Franny? Because you never know when you might stop for a pedicure—or a dumpster."

She had gathered orchids, sunflowers, and red ginger, and left behind phlox that she judged "past their prime." At home she would create a second tall flower arrangement and place it beside a mirror to create the illusion that the bouquet was twice its size.

"Professional floral arrangements are always thrown out too soon," she said. "These are still half fresh. Want some?" We walked home holding the dripping stems away from our clothes—our treasures worth $30 per stem, said Parsley, who knows the value of things. The blossoms lasted for one full week beyond their throw-out date. She was right yet again.

When I took on the task of feeding her parrot I had no idea it would become a daily gig that lasted a year and counting. I was perfectly happy to be of assistance and to assume increased responsibilities—her mail and banking—as the months wore on. I even planned to take her knives for sharpening, at her request, when the little cart with the man inside was parked on our block.

In search of her cooking secrets, I stumbled upon her private life. This poured out with my discovery of the steamer trunk. In the Eighties she had had an abortion. "It was for the best," she wrote. "It's not that I ever expected to have one—or an accidental pregnancy. But when it came to having an abortion, I didn't have to think about it for long. I was all for it." Parsley donates to Pro-Choice, as did her heroine, Julia Child, a champion of Planned Parenthood. "George Orwell would be Pro-Choice and Planned Parenthood big time if he were still around."

While she was away I haunted her apartment. There was that one locked diary, propped up alluringly on her bookshelf, right beside *Words Into Type* and *The Chicago Manual of Style*. Perhaps it would yield up her deepest secret. The steamer trunk had a partly open bottom drawer where Parsley kept her collection of power tools (sex toys). I jumped when one of them began to tick like a bomb. Respectfully, I closed that drawer back up; all of her secrets were contained in her cooking journal.

$\mathcal{H}$er first friends in New York showed Parsley the ropes—Diane Rye on the Upper West Side and Lindsay Salt in Chelsea. When the three friends, who saw a lot of each other, were married, they did complicated double and treble dates. They broke bread together at each other's various apartments, large and small.

Lindsay Salt, an artist, had an elegant presentation of food that Parsley copied. Everything was served on one platter: steamed broccoli, new potatoes, and roasted chicken, topped with a flower and a bouquet of fresh herbs. Visits often included food and families. Diane Rye, who started her own cooking school, had an aunt, Olive, who brought mango chutney to a family event. Parsley said, "I must have the recipe!"

Diane took Parsley aside and warned her that Olive never parts with her recipes—or when she must, she omits or alters one ingredient, to make sure that no one will ever duplicate the dish she made.

Parsley made Aunt Olive's mango chutney, and she could find nothing amiss. But it did somehow taste different when Olive made it, with the mystery ingredient restored—a star anis, a clove-studded tangerine?

Mango Chutney

5 large slices dried mango
2 cups fresh mango pieces
2 T veg oil
1 T sugar
2 dried chilis (or ½ tsp chili flakes)
1 tsp cumin
1 T curry powder
½ cup raisins or currants
½ cup cider vinegar
Reserved water from soaked mango
Sea salt to taste

Soak dried mango slices in 1 cup water for one hour or more. Reserve the water they soak in. Slice fresh mangos. Chop. Add oil and spices to a skillet, simmer. Add chopped dried and fresh mango. Add vinegar and reserved liquid, salt to taste, cook for 1 hour. Serve, and save leftovers in a sterilized, sealed jar in the refrigerator.

"There's a thin man inside every fat man," wrote George Orwell. "There's a fat woman inside every thin woman," wrote Parsley Cresswell.

Parsley was always prepared to have an affair right in her neighborhood—an easy commute and short taxi ride home. Single women need to keep such considerations in mind. She dated Juan Valdez, Josh Rogan, Orange Julius, Orville Redenbacher, and Francesco Rinaldi—and that's in a thirty-block radius including the opposite side of Central Park. Rarely does Parsley launch a real relationship.

Opera tenor Mario Provolone, handsome *gordo* from Moderna, Italy, a one-time star of City Opera, changed all that. It was like she grazed on high-priced hors d'oeuvres, then came a big, caloric entrée. Feathers of snow were falling on the night Mario accompanied Parsley home and proposed to her on the doorstep. Oh, I'm in love, Parsley thought, at least once every hour.

They lived beyond their means. She was a runner-up on the Best-Dressed List a year into their marriage. Yet her thrift-shop past is shown by her wedding gown: a white flowered frock she bought for twenty-five dollars at Encore consignment shop on Madison. She wrapped a length of tulle around her face and connected it in back, *et voila!* a bridal veil. She retailored the dress and started wearing it under a tight charcoal jacket to the office.

Parsley: married. She could not believe it. They tied the knot after a shockingly brief engagement of twelve months, and were married for about that long again. Who knows what heights of happiness they might have scaled if they gave it more time? (It's harder to fit into the timeline a fling with a rock legend she calls "Bob" or "Bobby" in her diaries, but who could only be the former Bobby Zimmerman.)

Mario moved into her cozy apartment up five flights of stairs. Most of his belongings were not at Parsley's but

DRAWING BY PHOEBE DINGWALL

in permanent storage (her idea), which was fortunate, because they did not last.

While Mario was around, he complimented her on her beauty, her décor, and on her green and leafy neighborhood. He had an image of the Upper East Side as being protected. There was chaos on the outside, but inside their select principality everything was in its proper place and a hot meal was provided.

"Meeting Parsley was like learning the Upper East Side secret handshake," said Mario, who was starring in *Falstaff* at the City Opera. Clearly, they had fun together. The newlyweds regularly absconded to different boroughs, usually by the 6, 7, and F trains, to Brooklyn and Queens, for the cheap romantic date. They liked to order freely in restaurants, which they could not do on the UES.

Mario and Parsley got to know the Conservatory Gardens and the tulip-islanded Park Avenue in spring. They loved their elite streets, and shopped for apartments along Fifth Avenue that they could never afford, just for the fantasy factor. They lived in the most celebrity-infested neighborhood in NYC and called it home.

The couple made enviable trips to La Scala and the Paris Opera. At the Met Opera's opening night, Parsley was photographed in her floral Carolina Herrera floor-length gown, and Mario in Armani Uomo, black tie, his hair slicked back, smiling like Mephistopheles in *Faust*, which, in fact, was one of his rôles. "How could I stay married to the devil?" Parsley posed. By all accounts she treated him like an angel and cooked his every whim, including **Angels on Horseback**. Use half-cooked bacon to wrap around shucked oysters (or scallops). Fasten with toothpicks. Broil or grill at high heat, until crispy on the outside. Serve hot, with lemon wedges, good bread, and chilled Pinot Noir.

DRAWING BY JENNIFER OLLE

"Art museums, restaurants, doormen in cute uniforms, majestic Central Park. Carnegie Hill has a rose-tinted view. It is historic, landmark-y, cinematic. Yet, the West Side is somehow brainier. There are more Ph.D.s per square block on the West Side, and more jillionaires on the UES. More nail and waxing salons." The UES was somehow her spiritual home—a gated community like Heaven.

Was it the Pinot Grigio at lunch at Table d'Hôte that made her head spin? She noticed that no one cooks on the Upper East Side. Oddly enough, she cooked more on the UES than she did in other neighborhoods. In the most expensive neighborhood in practically the entire world, Parsley had to tighten her belt to make ends meet. She went far afield to shop.

She kept her place too clean, like her neighbors with two housekeepers to Hoover. She cured herself of extreme tidying-up—Lady Macbeth syndrome—only when she hired someone to come in and clean the floors, and then, to sterilize the bathroom and kitchen and to vacuum all of the books on her shelves of dust. She offered her housekeeper a musical selection and, if the weather was hot, cold beer.

"Am I asking you to do too much?" Parsley asked anxiously.

"You kidding?" the very thorough cleaner said. "Blanche Cart has me shampoo her dog while I'm at it!"

When eating at a restaurant, Parsley discretely wipes the tines of her fork and dabs hand sanitizer on her fingertips. At home, she removes footwear at the door and washes her hands with hot water. She loves glove weather for its extra layer of germ protection.

Apart from an immersion blender, she has no other electrical appliances. A French toasting pan works as her toaster. The kitchen is neo-Luddite. Copper fish pots on the wall are mise-en-scène—polished regularly, hardly used. There is no countertop coffee maker. To make coffee, she pours hot water into a cone and thermos. Cabinet doors are studded with *New Yorker* cartoons and postcards.

When I moved to New York from Weehawken, Parsley offered to show me the ropes. She visited my apartment and commented that I should spruce up that temporary mountain of boxes with a sari, and she lent me a turquoise and cobalt one, beaded and embroidered. It's still there. I could tell already that she was more organized than even I, a C.P.A., could be. This should bode well for her in prison, where I can imagine her minimal objects (comb, soap) beautifully arranged.

As a housewarming present, she brought over her famous, simple Onion Pie, decorated with asparagus and black olives.

Onion Pie

   1 pie crust (commercial or homemade)
   2 Spanish onions, chopped and caramelized in butter and olive oil
   1½ cups grated Wisconsin cheese

Preheat the oven to 350°F. Slice the onions and caramelize on medium-slow, adding a pinch of salt and pinch of sugar to hurry the process. (It still takes at least ten minutes standing at the stove and stirring.)

Prick the bottom of the pie crust with a fork and bake it for ten minutes.

Mix cooked onions with grated cheese. Spoon it into the par-baked pie shell. Decorate with asparagus, red pepper strips, and black olives, or practically anything else, before returning to the oven for 20 minutes or so. It's OK if the crust gets burnt.

Pie Crust

   8 T cold unsalted butter, in tablespoon-size pieces
   1½ cups flour
   ½ tsp salt
   ½ tsp sugar
   ½ cup cold vegetable shortening

About ¼ cup ice water

Blend butter into the flour and other ingredients with fingers and the heel of your hands. Roll out onto a floured surface. Butter pan before adding the dough. Make a ball of leftover dough and freeze to make a small tart another day.

*W*hen I opened the door to Parsley's apartment an updraft of cold air, like a ghost, shook the chandelier. The parrot, an African Grey, was quiet, mysteriously enough. I waited, frozen, for him to speak. "Hel-lo," he called out. We greeted one another. I put his colorful rainforest blend seed assortment into his Edo-era Japanese pottery, inside the door of the frilly Victorian birdcage that he occupies at the center of Parsley's studio apartment.

"Hel-lo. Good-bye." I said.

"Hellohellohellohello!" Gougère did exuberant twirls and shook with excitement. Then he let out a pterodactyl cry.

I clearly enunciated each syllable of the parrot's spookiest line: "Are you OK?"

"OK," he said, nodding his head. Then, in Parsley's flat Midwestern accent, in her exact alto voice, he asked, *"Are you OK?"*

I shivered at the uncanniness of Gougère and tried to form an answer. He looked at me expectantly, hanging on to my every word. When Parsley went to Europe she left Gougère with Pomegranate Hades-Taylor. Her bird came back to her knowing Hamlet's "To be-e or *not* to be-e. *Tha-at* is the ques-tion," and Bette Davis's "What a dump!"

It was then that out of the corner of my eye I saw the black mouse skate along the floorboards and flatten himself (one always hopes the mouse is a male) beneath the door of the walk-in closet. I bristled—but if I had screamed, certainly Gougère would have too, and our combined shrieks would have caused a neighbor to call 911. With Parsley away in special circumstances, her neighbors and I tried to keep her absence on the down low.

I took the matter in hand, a responsibility for which an MBA from Princeton did nothing to prepare me. Returning in daylight I put out traps. For Parsley, anything: three mousetraps with various lures, per her instructions over the prison phone—one baited with bread, one peanut butter, one cheddar cheese. "It is your patriotic duty to buy more cheese from Wisconsin," she urged me. Using my language, she taught that a refrigerator stocked with cheese, frozen peas, onions and butter represented a "net benefit" in one's life, because they gave more possibilities to dinner than anything else.

Again when I visited Gougère, I saw the beast sweep under the door, and I froze. I walked across the boudoir, and for the first time, I touched the closet's tasseled doorknob.

The closet door flew open, and a pink incandescent bulb flicked on, illuminating Parsley's carefully curated and labeled accessories and clothing. In the middle stood a tall steamer trunk that contained stuffed drawers and pigeonholes. The departments revealed further recipes from places and points, poems and love letters. She saved recipe-stuffed travel journals and tax-time receipts from B. Altman, Café des Artistes, Hanratty's Jazz Dinner Club, etc., and menus. I was surprised to find she had Metropolitan Opera series tickets for years after she divorced tenor Mario, and in spite of spotty freelance employment. Files held her résumés, love letters, suicide note(s), hypothetical Oscar acceptance speech, unfinished screenplays, last will and testament. Slipped in between were pressed wildflowers and flattened Japanese maple leaves.

The steamer trunk was presided over by a blown-up, framed picture of a young man with curly hair and a younger Parsley, signed, "Thanks for 'Country Pie,' Yours, Bob" Could that be *the* Bob she drapes her arm around in the black-and-white photo? She always did hate Joan Baez. "Baez is a four-letter word," she remarked while we sat on her leafy terrace drinking frozen daiquiris made from limeade concentrate, *"An old family recipe,"* she said, or was it **Tintos de Verano** (red wine with Sprite or 7-Up, ice, fresh mint, lemon slice)?

Pulling open a neat drawer of the trunk, a moth flew out (note to self to call the exterminator). Leaving it for the moment, shutting off the wardrobe light, I shook my head and said. "Oh, Parsley, Parsley, Parsley." The parrot repeated back, *"Oh!* Parsley, Parsley... *Oh!"*

I had a check to post, and as I prepared to leave her apartment and go outside, I borrowed her coat. It was a Zandra Rhodes, bright yellow, and as I walked toward Madison Avenue to the mailbox, a man in profile against a streetlamp called out, "Parsley my love, is that you?" I froze. A tall, good-looking doorman with an Irish accent (I recognized him from 96th St), in a dark green uniform with gold trim and a modified top hat ran toward me with an expectant smile. When he was close enough to kiss my mouth, he drew back. "Ah, sorry, miss, I thought you were someone else!"

Seamus Farl was distressed to learn that Parsley was "out of town for an extended time." He said he'd taken in a package for her, as he had in the past. (Since there is no doorman at our brownstone, it's safer to arrange to have an important package delivered to a neighbor's doorman lobby.) "So, might you be willing to take it for her?"

"Certainly," I said. The box was quite heavy!

"Books, I'm sure," Farl explained, and gallantly offered to carry it back for me when he got off work. "We share a love of great literature, Parsley and I," he said in his lovely Cork accent. "Otherwise, I'd never have a chance with such a great woman. Literature and poetry—we have that." He wiped a tear from his eye.

Home and alone, I opened the Fresh Direct "box of books" to find bricks of hundred-dollar bills. It was then that I had the discomfiting thought that Parsley had been complicit in a pyramid, or at least a money laundering, scheme. Or could it be, giving Parsley the benefit of the doubt, that an old friend, a hedge-fund manager, donated a defense fund anonymously? Parsley would look on the bright side of any gift! The next opportunity for a prison visit, I found a way to broach the subject.

It was a fall day when we met, and that was reflected in the tiny windows of the visitors' "lounge", as we called it. It's always a fresh surprise to me that Parsley Cresswell has gone in for a dramatic change of style, for how could she not? No more the fashion plate, she had to make do with tidy hair prematurely gray, great bone structure, and the perfect posture of a ballerina. Were it not for the orange jumpsuit, Parsley might have been an actress in the theatre who'd just removed her makeup and false eyelashes. It goes without saying Parsley knew how to make prison garb look timeless and chic. Had she gained a bit of weight? Might have. It looked good on her. I always thought she was too thin before.

"Parsley," I said, in a moment I had rehearsed in front of the mirror, trying to make it sound natural, as a guard listens in to our conversation. "Parsley, the Irish doorman from around the corner, Farl, took in an order for you from Fresh Direct."

Nonplussed, she said, "Oh yeah? What was in it?"

"Arugula," I said. "Romaine and spinach, kale. *Tender.*"

Her eyes widened slightly, an eyebrow was raised, but her body language remained relaxed. I'm pretty sure she was oblivious.

"What shall I do with it?" I asked.

"Put it in your refrigerator. Then make a nice salad for yourself."

DRAWING BY PHOEBE DINGWALL

Over time, Parsley worked at practically every magazine on the newsstand. The fashion daily where she wound
up for several years was an oasis of potted paperwhites
and hyacinths and silk Hermès scarves. "All manner of
swag was showered on the editors," Parsley wrote in her
journal, with her characteristic excellent subject-verb
agreement. Covered in complimentary cosmetics, Parsley
edited thousands of what were called lifestyle articles. Her
boss, Winston, warned her, "Watch out! These people
on the society pages—they'll soon feel like your family."
Parsley laughed.

Too much salt is just as bad as too much sugar, Parsley
found out at the fashion daily. "How can you do that to
yourself?" says her pencil-slim co-editor when she returns
from lunch with an ice-cream bar. But Parsley grew up
in the Midwest and believed that she experienced a form
of hypoglycemia if she didn't get a constant infusion of
calcium in the form of milk, cheese or ice cream, especially in the winter.

She typed in her computer password: Aloha. She
printed out her e-mails and filed a hard copy. She learned
to walk by leading with the blades of her hips, and to turn

the corner like a runway model, while glancing back. Style was her mission. Fashion was what she wore, back before the Gap and its khaki uniform, back before everyone started wearing black. French fries were her favorite indulgence. She tried instead to order the Salade Niçoise.

Salade Niçoise

Seared tuna or canned tuna in olive oil. Empty tuna and oil over butter lettuce and blend. Arrange on a plate, surrounded by boiled red potatoes, blanched green beans, 1 hard-boiled egg, black olives, chopped onions. Sprinkle with capers, freshly ground pepper, and chopped parsley and tarragon. Drizzle with vinaigrette or **balsamic reduction** (2 cloves chopped garlic, browned in a dot of olive oil. Add 1 cup balsamic vinegar, bring to a watched boil and turn down to simmer, stirring occasionally, until the vinegar has reduced to about ⅓ cup).

"*A* purge is as good as a splurge." To compensate her great joy in eating, she sometimes took a break with a one-day juice and soup fast—usually midweek. When fasting, she ended her day early, with Compline at Nine, a penitential prayer. It made her feel, she said, like a fasting saint, pure and cleansed, sharp as a tack. "I can see my image on a holy card, in a gown by Worth."

Parsley kept addictive food in the freezer. "That way you won't be tempted to eat it suddenly. It has to thaw out." Frozen pistachios, dark chocolate and homemade granola bars. And because she is finicky about the freshness of the nuts in her cereal, she mixes her own granola and keeps it in the freezer, the better to resist it.

She listens to French and Italian tapes while her granola defrosts and she does stomach curls. "I tell myself that there's nothing I want to eat. When I diet, I'm just not in the mood for food."

Whether onstage, backstage, or sitting in the audience directing a rehearsal, playwright Pomegranate Hades-Taylor, our neighbor, brought to the theatre a very fresh salad that contained everything but the kitchen sink. "So that I can feel virtuous for about five minutes," Pom said. Virtuous Salad may be served undressed, which only increases its virtue.

Virtuous Salad

Fresh ginger grated onto tuna seared or canned, with green grapes or cherry tomatoes cut in half, 1 or 2 grated carrots, celery, green apple, toasted walnuts, olives, artichoke hearts, hearts of palm, cucumber, radish, red pepper flakes, and anything else at hand, with a pinch of salt or **yogurt and mayo dressing** (1 clove minced garlic, 1 T olive oil, 1 T rice vinegar, ½ cup plain yogurt, 2 T mayonnaise, chopped dill, chopped parsley, chopped sundried tomato slice, pepper and salt).

*T*he bliss of having an entire weekend ahead was best enjoyed while she was married. Sunday was their day of rest, then Mario's voice coach schedule shifted and it was Tuesdays that he was free to spend entirely with his beloved Parsley, when she was between jobs. Art museums were open for free on Tuesdays. They went to a museum a bit before noon, then returned to have a leisurely **Late Lunch** of salad, soup, cheese, and baguette (heated for 10 minutes in a 350°F oven), with chilled Sauvignon Blanc. Even on a budget, they managed to be wine snobs. Neither drank Chardonnay, unless it was French Chardonnay. In the time before Malbec and Shiraz, Chianti was their red of choice.

Although she was thrifty to begin with, when she moved to the UES she sharpened her penny-pinching ways. This was fortunate, because Mario was a spendthrift. One year into her marriage, dumping him felt like a budgetary measure, said Parsley. It forced her to cook, because while married, Mario was a stellar househusband who did all of the cooking. He kept their freezer stocked with a bottle of vodka, four ice cube trays filled with filtered water, croissants and baguette, *petite pois*, unsalted butter, and a couple of lobster tails.

Parsley and Mario parted amicably. ("Why draw things out? we agreed.") She had learned a lot from him, including "Quando m'en vo," "Toréador," and his Sicilian mother's recipe for Bolognese. Here's a soup for Tuesdays with Mario. He added a smattering of red pepper flakes and finely minced parsley before serving it. Vermicelli sometimes replaced or joined the lentils toward the end of the cooking cycle.

Coconut Lentil Soup

3 cups boiling water or stock
1 ½ cup lentils, rinsed
1 T olive oil
1 onion, diced
4 cloves garlic, minced
2 T ginger, minced
1 carrot, diced
1 celery stalk, diced
½ tsp red pepper flakes, more for garnish
1 tsp cumin
1 pinch coriander
1 T red curry paste
1 can coconut milk
Yogurt
Fresh herbs

While lentils plump in boiling water, heat the oil in a

frying pan and sauté onion, garlic, ginger, carrot and celery. Add seasonings and curry paste. Add mixture to the lentils when lentils are partway cooked. Add the coconut milk and heat. Serve with a dab of yogurt and the garnish of chopped herbs and red pepper flakes.

"*V*iv Clicquot hosted a spring fundraiser in her ten-thousand square foot, 'classic six' overlooking the reservoir. Little salads with caviar and edible flowers were nestled in radicchio cups, served on silver platters by white-gloved butlers. Champagne in flutes. A mezzo-soprano, accompanied by a Steinway and a cellist. Smoked salmon and caviar on Ripples potato chip, with a spot of crème fraiche and dill," Parsley wrote, with a pencil illustration of this fine hors d'oeuvre.

"The best fundraising trick," according to Viv, "is a good view."

The party was more fun since Viv's husband was no longer around. When Viv married him, she was forced to sign a pre-nup, with a "sunset clause" stating the pre-nup terms would be invalid after thirty years of marriage. "Considering that he was seventy-plus, it was optimistic of him," Parsley wrote.

Viv retaliated with a pre-nup of her own, which included a bad-boy clause, as her new husband, old as he was, was an inveterate skirt chaser and easily caught. She hired an unknown actress, Gisela Feijoada, to wear a maid costume and to clean their house, hoping to lure the old man into an affair and a divorce—maybe a heart attack. Fortunate for Gisela, who would have suffered qualms otherwise, he expired all on his own while walking the dog.

Quiche, a French bulldog, barked for help, eliciting a doorman with a cell phone who called for an ambulance, too late, leaving Viv a wealthy widow, with money enough to hire Gisela to return and cook a weekly dinner party for eight, since her cooking was "gourmet," as Herb de Provence put it. "Gisela hopes to meet a film director at Viv's gatherings," Parsley said. "Viv always promises to have one on the invitation list."

Viv cornered me after Parsley's arrest.

"How is Parsley taking it?" Viv asked, her beautiful face lit with an indulgent smile.

The disparity between rich and poor on the Upper East Side should further one's understanding of the world, but somehow it does not. Gisela is often given Viv's cast-off designer clothing, and though it is never meant as an insult, Gisela heard the genuine surprise in Viv's voice when she said, "You look better in that dress than I did!"

Gisela said to Parsley and me, "*Of course,* I look better in her clothes!"

This ubiquitous dessert is from Gisela's native Brazil. Parsley noted, "Brigadiero looks a little different at everybody's house, but you can count on it to taste exactly the same. Such predictability is rare in national cuisines."

Brazilian desserts are stovetop, for hot temperatures, and are taught by word of mouth, with measurements that are conveniently easy to remember.

Brigadiero Stir an 8 oz. can of sweetened condensed milk in a frying pan, with a heat-resistant spatula, for up to a half hour. Put on some good music! Stir in 1 T butter and 3 T cocoa. Stir until thickened, then pull from the stove and drop onto a buttered slab. When it has cooled down, butter your hands and roll balls (15 to 20), in pine nuts, chopped pistachios, coconut, chocolate sprinkles, powdered sugar, etc.

"*Y*ou can go to a different restaurant every night for two years in Manhattan without dining at the same place twice. New Yorkers eat like rock stars." What she would not give to eat in a restaurant every night!

With inflation, restaurant dinners became rare and gala invitations fewer. At a fundraiser in view of the Empire State and the Chrysler buildings, a gloved waiter hovered with a silver appetizer tray. "*Foie gras*? No, thank you!" Parsley said in earshot of her PETA friend.

She moonlighted as a restaurant critic and carried away copious doggie bags with provender for another meal, and she became an expert at making even third meals out of restaurant scraps by adding chopped celery and onions. Last night's baked potato made a superb frittata with scallions, eggs, a fine grating of extra sharp Wisconsin aged cheddar, and a dash of Tabasco sauce. But this is not to say she wasn't very fussy.

Elaine's Restaurant rated just two Parsley Stars. "The food lacked all pretension, but so did the waiters. Gelatinous spaghetti served with a sauce like cat food. Overpriced wine. However, I sat at a table next to a celebrity divorce lawyer and a four-time Oscar nominee, close enough to eavesdrop on juicy conversation, so the night was a roaring success."

She felt it her duty to review any new restaurant on the Upper East Side, as if to coax it into submission to her taste and price-range. "Can cooking for oneself ever be quite as memorable as a meal in a posh restaurant?" she wrote in her notebook, beside remarks on the noise level, ambience and décor of Bistro du Nord.

The waiter had just brought Parsley's plate before the hush fell. An older woman, thin as a rail, coiffed and well turned out, sitting three tables away, dropped dead after her second martini.

While the young medics administered the kiss of life, Parsley's fragrant lobster—combined with her extreme hunger after a full day at work—made her cry out for a morsel of fish, and she tried as best she could to keep from eating. Tears sprang from her eyes. She was hardly able to control herself and turned her head away from the quickening chaos, to delicately steal, with manicured fingertips, bits of buttered lobster into her mouth, hoping that no one noticed.

"May I have a doggie bag?" she always asked at the end of the meal, though she hasn't had a dog for years. She served fish pie the next night, invited her next-door neighbor, and recounted her restaurant adventure.

Fish Pie

Puff pastry, thawed
1½ lb. scallops and shrimp
      (lobster, optional)
1 T olive oil
1 T butter
1 clove garlic, chopped
½ large onion, sliced
1 rib celery, deveined and diced
1 carrot, small dice
1½ cup mixed chopped mushrooms
1 cup heavy cream
⅓ cup milk
¼ cup lemon juice
Nutmeg
2 T chopped parsley and dill

Unfold thawed puff pastry on a floured surface and cut to fit the cooking dish. Refrigerate until ready to use. Boil shrimp and gently sauté the scallops. Remove from pan and refrigerate. Add butter and oil to a pan and garlic, onion, celery, carrot, and mushrooms. Combine heavy cream, milk, and lemon juice in a bowl, grate nutmeg over the top, and stir once or twice while it thickens. Put fish in greased cooking dish, cover with herbs, vegetables and sauce. Place the refrigerated puff pastry over the pie and cut a fish shape for steam to escape. Bake at 350°F for 35 minutes or until crust rises and browns.

*I*nvite Parsley to your house for dinner and she'd keep you on her holiday card list for ten years. She posted cards to arrive with the new year. Her economical system for making them out was to address and stamp all the envelopes first. She kept a moistened sponge in a Spode dish beside her, so that she will not have to lick the envelopes or stamps.

Her annual New Year's bash (not quite a cocktail party, not quite a sit-down dinner) was black tie. "Sequins always look best by candlelight," she wrote, "and candles look better with sequins." She bought a gold sequined shrug cardigan and wore it on top of a black office dress when she had a party after work.

"A countdown at midnight is de rigueur." Then she and her guests run out to Central Park with hot drinks in mugs to watch the midnight run.

From her 1999 food diary: "For New Year's Eve, I will be sculpting an **Edible Centerpiece** of a clock, lining an 8-inch round spring form cake pan with Saran Wrap, then filling it 1 inch or more with cooked and vinegared sushi rice. Refrigerate, then remove from pan, cover with smoked salmon and a border of red salmon caviar, minced green pepper, and dill. With chives and black olives make a clock face at midnight. Encircle with lemon slices."

How did she keep that holiday glow right through to Epiphany or Twelfth Night? Sometimes the end of the year holidays were not enough for Parsley, and she continued to bake and cook like a mad scientist into the new year.

She considered Oscar Night the official end to the holiday season and her second favorite holiday after Thanksgiving. She served only popcorn and cheap BYOB, too excited by the gowns to cook. "It's just outrageous that there is no awards ceremony for opera!" Mario used to grumble.

"Should auld acquaintances be forgot? Certainly, if you want to. It's your party," was Parsley's advice. Invite no more than eight, including oneself. Six, she thinks, is the ideal number. She calls this rule the Joy of Six.

"If you invite more than five or six, have a cocktail party. Serve substantial appetizers hot and cold, shrimp in one form or another, and cheese and crackers. Introduce guests to one another. Someone should be assigned to keep glasses filled." She played a CD of Jellyroll Morton while she executed dainty salmon sandwiches, decorated with a piped rosette of cream cheese and a frond of dill.

As opposed to the cocktail party, the dinner party is a culinary rite. Plans to have people over means creative tension for Parsley. She polishes the silver, writes out a seating plan and finds out everyone's food allergies and restrictions.

She kept a fantasy dinner party list that one year included Michael Jackson. Most of the guests were artists or writers—Fran Lebowitz, Mario Vargas Llosa, Pauline Kael, David Bowie, Johnny Depp, Jean-Pierre Léaud, Marlon Brando. Vivienne Westwood and Kate Moss appeared, Yoko Ono, Mother Teresa of Calcutta, James De La Vega, Lady Gaga, the Queen, Julia Child, the Dalai Lama, Fidel Castro, Bill and Hillary Clinton, Jimmy and Rosalynn Carter, Barack and Michelle Obama, and Aung San Suu Kyi. And did I say Bob Dylan? Bette Midler made her ideal dinner party list year after year.

Parsley said that she would have it catered. With fascinating guests, she would like to have someone cook and plate a sit-down dinner. More than likely there would be a guest on a restrictive diet that she could not suit, and she would hand him her folder of carryout menus to pick out some food, any food, that he can eat. On the Upper East Side, the world is your oyster as regards carryout menus from every country.

*I*t was not so much that a man was "Parsley's type." She had no type, though she was clear about who was not her type. Married with children, she said, was a deal breaker, as was cradle robber—for a long time she considered any man ten years her senior a geezer. He couldn't be younger by that much either. She wanted a boyfriend who was employed, competent, and preferably, one who owned a car so they could race away on weekends.

A different race, a different religion was not a deal breaker with Parsley. She felt no sense of social stigma about dating men who were not like her, but then, Parsley considered herself to be a member of every race, every religion.

She hooked up with a West African, educated at the Sorbonne, most dapper, who ran an NGO. Canelo taught her fish stew and took her shopping along Ninth Avenue. She documented their iconic meals. They shared recipes learned from their mothers—an intimate activity if there ever was one. Soon he was whisking up popovers (*The Upper East Side Cookbook,* Vol. 1) at the drop of a hat, and she could make a vegetable mash called Fufu.

She met some of Canelo's Senegalese friends. "So, have

you noticed the common quality in Senegalese men?" he asked. Parsley thought. "Do you mean, very black skin?" Canelo said, "Yes, but not that. You, of all people, Parsley! Did you not recognize that we have wonderful fashion sense?" "Oh, yes," said Parsley. "Yes, indeed."

After he moved away, Canelo continued to keep in touch with PC. In the lovely time they were together, he taught her Chicken Mahfah (pronounced mah-fay), which she translated into Peanut Chicken Soup. He called it Ancestor Soup when he made it on Forebear Friday, which he devotes to Skype-ing with far flung cousins, editing family photos and digitalizing them.

Peanut Chicken Soup

6-10 small red or fingerling potatoes
Olive oil
2 chicken breasts and two chicken thighs, bones removed and chopped
2 cloves garlic, chopped
Fresh ginger, minced
1 carrot, chopped
2 ribs celery, chopped
1 tsp chili seasoning
1 tsp curry
1 T cumin
½ cup peanut butter
Mint
Julienned peeled cucumber
Lime wedges

Boil potatoes for 15-20 minutes. In a heavy soup pan, fry chicken pieces in olive oil, garlic and ginger. Add carrots and boiled potatoes, celery, and enough chicken stock to cover. Add chili, curry, and cumin. Last of all add peanut butter. Garnish with mint, cucumber, and lime wedges. Serve with Tabasco or red-pepper sauce on the side. (Tip: Okra, zucchini, eggplant, cabbage and more can be added to this dish.)

Drawing by Catherine Stock

*P*arsley looks through old pictures and tosses out the ones in which she looks fat or less than exuberantly happy. Then she tosses out some clothes from her closet to make room for new ones. Rather, new old ones. Because she cannot shop at Prada, she goes to church rummage sales and charity shops.

At the Church of St. Thomas More, she found a bronzed baby shoe to grow chives in. She went first to the tables selling kitchen things. Her weakness for plates was gratified easily because she did not mind chips. It was amazing to her when she could actually buy some cheap, precious old thing—a gooseneck lamp or a cross-stitched tablecloth from Finland.

Parsley claimed she does all her designer clothes shopping in Third Avenue thrift shops, but it is at the church rummage sales on Park, Madison, and Fifth, where she really scores. She waits in line with other ruthless shoppers to be the first inside. "When I step into the Church of the Heavenly Rest, a cathedral with a rose window, I am there for a rummage sale, but I feel like an infidel celebrant heading toward a pagan ritual."

She convinced herself that the Eighties cocktail dress she bought at St. James Episcopal was just as chic, in fact, better made, than anything she could buy in a store today. Whenever she needed to remind herself of the superiority of her find, she looked at the seams, finished with a slip-stitch. At Brick Presbyterian, she got a winter coat for $20 that had a wrinkled $20 bill stuffed deep in the pocket. "Only on the Upper East Side," she said.

Another pleasure of the church bazaar was the bakery and home-made preserves—mango chutney and the excellent, not too sweet, crunchy cranberry relish from Park Avenue United Methodist that was the star of a Riverside Park picnic in late November for which she made Thanksgiving turkey sandwiches with cranberry relish on caraway rye.

She returned to the Park Avenue church year after year for the relish, only to find it missing in late 2005. When Parsley asked about it, the woman behind the home-baked goods counter widened her eyes and said theatrically, "She died and took her recipe with her!"

She walked along the avenue at night and peered into the windows at her neighbors' enviable art collections: the Barnett Newman in the living room with the white leather sectionals, the Philip Pearlstein figures, and the Francis Bacon sides of beef. She always paused at the address designed by architect Risotto Piano and decorated by art dealer Cherry Gagosian, in awe of the Cindy Sherman portrait, the Soutine elegantly dressed lady, and a Flemish Old Master Annunciation with *craquelure*—Parsley examined them carefully through pearl-encrusted opera glasses.

Plum and Herb de Provence had a painting by Belgian artist Marshmaleaux of a partly nude woman, which hung prominently over their fireplace and had been in the family since before the Great Depression. After the 2008 market collapse, the 1905 painting was sold.

"Not for the money. We just couldn't afford the insurance any longer," Plum said. Before the auction house took the painting away she had a copyist do an exact reproduction of the lady on the bed wearing only a feather hair ornament. "I like the copy more than the original," Plum said—stoically.

"There's a new stoicism on the Upper East Side," Parsley wrote in her journal, feeling like she was standing in the VIP lounge. Her favorite comment on living among art collectors comes from her late Upper East Side neighbor, Andy Warhol, who said no matter how much money you have you can't get a better bottle of Coca-Cola.

Her hero George Orwell said rich and poor are "differentiated by their incomes and nothing else, and the average millionaire is only the average dishwasher dressed in a new suit." Some neighbors bought dresses worth more than the combined GNP of a couple of the least developed countries. Capital gains taxes of 14% allowed one to purchase a house, put a line of credit on it, and buy a private plane, and others unexpectedly hit the skids.

Parsley found antiques in the neighbors' trash and went foraging on the nights that furniture was left on the curb. Her apartment was decorated with cast-offs—a curved desk, leather Windsor chair, a patchwork ottoman, and a miniature grand piano for a child that served as her cocktail table. There's nothing wrong with leftovers. Her classic **Vegetable Soup**, a pint of which could always be defrosted from the freezer, was made from frozen petite peas, chopped herbs, and leftover vegetables, including potatoes, beans and legumes. Blend, using an immersion blender, with chicken stock and a pinch of curry.

On a trip to Detroit for Lindsay Salt's wedding, Parsley sampled the legendary Detroit Chili Dog late one night, in its fluorescent-lit purveyor. With the first bite, Parsley's expert palate told her that the chili topping was indeed spiked with curry powder. No one has ever been able to crack the secret formula to **Parsley's Chili**, made just like everybody else's, though with a pinch of curry powder, one star anise, and a page of konbu seaweed among the ingredients.

*A*fternoon sun makes any room look good. As golden light slanted across her desk PC checked e-mail. She felt the flicker of a memory, a déjà vu vibe. Late afternoon was the best time of day to recall that dream from the night before, she told me, and to set something simmering on the stove, and for her to think of interesting UES neighbors—including the insufferable Blanche Cart, who bragged of having set up a spy-cam in a bathroom to see which of her staff was stealing from the medicine cabinet.

"What did the 'thief' steal?" Parsley asked Viv.

"Well, that's just what I asked!" said Viv Clicquot. "She claims it was the Midol she needed for her PMS— isn't that Blanche for you?"

Blanche posed as being both younger and more loaded than she really was. She pledged major funds to her charities: opera, ballet, and the nascent Abercrombie and Fitch modeling school for men. "We all need another hero," Blanche was quoted as saying in *Vogue*, misquoting Tina Turner. The charities called to remind her of her generous pledge, when the money did not arrive. Blanche said, "It will come. Rest assured." Blanche was wined and dined and courted again. Many await money she has promised them still.

When the *Daily News* broke the story, it was already ten years into her scam, and the paper called Blanche for her comment. She told the reporter, without a trace of insouciance, "As I said, I will be getting the funds."

Parsley saw it as a Mark Twain maneuver, like the painted fence.

Parsley stirred the pot and told me about the dandy, Papriko McDonalds, in his tartan suit, and top fashion journalist, Lime Yaeger, whose dress, hair and makeup she greatly admired. Also very well turned out in her opinion, in oilskin jacket, cowboy fringe and hat, editor and writer Gordon Dish. She talked about the May-December couples, the unlikely couples, and the simply rich—like the neighbors who have a Jeff Koons Puppy in their back-yard—and Freixenet and Gelata Popova. The wife with her faint moustache, was neither the more female nor the more male. The husband was theatrically non-macho. Parsley was not at all surprised when Gelata brought to a hen party a dessert made by husband Freixenet.

Olhos de Sogra (Mother-in-Law's Eyes)

1 pound Medjool dates
1 cup water
1 cup sugar
1 cup coconut, grated (or unsweetened)
2 large egg yolks

½ tsp vanilla
Cloves, for garnish

Carefully split dates and remove seeds by hand, leaving the shape of a boat. Date filling: Put 1 cup each of sugar, water and coconut in a sauce pan and stir over medium heat until thickened. Remove from heat and cool. Whip egg yolks and add, with vanilla. Return to the stove and cook for a bit longer. Remove and cool. Butter your hands and roll an "eyeball" to fit into the prune. Roll the filled prune in the remaining sugar. Dot with a clove (to be removed before eating). Serve in small paper baking cups.

*P*arsley Cresswell visited my apartment and remarked on the splendid view. With all of those windows, this would be a great place for a telescope, she remarked. "Spying on your neighbors seems almost old-fashioned," she said, "now that it's been replaced by internet porn."

"Perhaps apartments sell for more if there are exhibitionists in the view. Realtors might promote them," I quipped.

"REE-uhl-ter," Parsley corrected me.

"That's what I said," I said.

"No you didn't. You said REEL-uh-ter."

Though she could seem la-de-dah, Parsley wasn't one to speak badly of people—certainly not of her exes. She was good to everybody, and always good for a free meal. Even for a one-night stand she cooks breakfast.

She could be elliptical. A neighbor reported that she saw Parsley on her terrace doing yoga by the light of the full moon—in the nude. When I asked about it she flatly denied everything. But then, and here is something I like about Parsley, she usually tells the truth.

She did a double take, looking genuinely surprised.

"Um, maybe I did! Yes, probably one moonlit night I did yoga on the terrace in the nude. Sure, that sounds like something I would do."

There was an air of suspense about Parsley. "Frankly, I'd rather not talk about it," when I asked the relatively impersonal question, "Where did you go for lunch, Parsley?"

She looked askance. "You didn't see us near the window at the restaurant, *did you?*" "You? And who?" I pried. "Me and... *the married man*! I should know that I can't take him anywhere."

"No, no! I didn't see you!" I insisted, although I had. They were sitting in the window at Demarchelier restaurant on 86th and Madison. You'd have to be blind not to notice Parsley in a leopard print dress, red mules, and red floppy hat. It didn't matter whom she was with. If she was with somebody else's husband, I could never force myself to judge Parsley. I was open to thinking that morally she was on the up and up, whatever she did.

"If that man left his wife, she'd send me a thank-you note," Parsley said, emphatically.

She claimed to brush up on her high-school *français* by watching the French news on cable TV. In truth, it was by checking her horoscope in *Vogue* Paris that she practiced French. If you should want to discuss destiny in French, Parsley Cresswell is your go-to woman. "*Tout le monde vous aime.*"

She clipped her *Town and Country* horoscope when it

was good. She read, "The stars this month offer enchant-
ment and a reality check; magic with an audit on the side.
Eventually the piper must be paid." So true. "Some days
it's like getting a Valentine: 'Sagittarius sometimes likes to
be alone. But be advised you have a secret admirer. No one
can resist your killer smile'."

That night, walking a neighbor's dog, she locked eyes
with a handsome, haggard looking, single man who'd
stepped outside an AA meeting to smoke.

Parsley had looked into the stained glass windows of
the Fifth Avenue church where the meeting was taking
place, and she envied the people inside their intimacy,
their camaraderie.

She and her new friend, Quince, drank tea and shared
a late-night Green Pie and told their life stories before he
took a cab home and vowed to call her the next day. After
he left, she sat outdoors in the lotus position.

*I*n the 21st Century there has been a new green economy on the Upper East Side: fewer limos, more people taking the bus. It began to be easy to get a table at any coveted restaurant, and restaurant "small plates" were introduced as though there was something hip or redeeming about ordering an expensive, small portion. Around this time Parsley started topping up her wine glass with water, when no one was looking, to make one drink last longer. She read that Thoreau drank only water and decided to aspire to that.

People were staying home and re-learning to cook. It was around this time that Parsley seriously dusted off her skills—and it was as a home chef that I first admired my neighbor. Most New Yorkers simply order carryout when the temp hits one hundred, but Parsley cooked constitutionally, ever since she took up her "austerity plan", as she called it—not that she has ever been on any other kind of plan. When she was alone she cooked in only an apron.

On the Upper East Side professional gardeners plant the window boxes. The piercing sound of birdsong heralds the day, before the construction drills begin at 8 a.m. on the dot. New homeowners in the area traditionally do a so-called "gut" renovation before they move in. Construction sounds are everywhere, like at a barn raising or a modern civil war.

In nearby Central Park, love is in the air. Neighbors have not lost their winter tans but are already opening up their summerhouses in the Hamptons. It is Sword of Damocles to be living on the Upper East Side, she said. (Once Google came about, Parsley was able to sort out that it *was* Sword of Damocles—not Occam's razor—that represented the circumstances of being on the UES.) Yet, she felt it halfway reassuring to be living among the super rich—even if she used the service entrance, their stability rubbed off on her.

The early money lessons Parsley received on the farm ensured that she never lighted the oven for just one item. The better use of energy was to turn on the oven to cook a succession of items. If it's too much for dinner, she'll have leftovers to heat in the microwave. She never makes just one pie, but two, freezing one.

November 1 and April 1, her seven boxes of clothes are opened, emptied of the new season, and filled with the season just past. She took out and changed her winter sleepwear (mukluks, flannel grannies and bedroom-silk mandarin collar pajamas) to her summer nightie wardrobe of baby-dolls and matching thongs, floaty caftans and sarongs. "Like a maple tree changing colors," she wrote.

According to her food diary, she did a DIY renovation (fresh paint, new drapes and throw cushions) "rather than hire Mario Buatta again." I was skeptical that her place was ever professionally decorated, but I liked Parsley Cresswell so much that I didn't even mind that she told me comforting white lies—for what is more comforting than money, or even imaginary associations with money?

A bookworm as a child, books continued to be her friends. Parsley belonged to the New York Society Library, a subscription library founded in 1754, with women among the charter members. She considered it her club, and went directly to the second floor reading room to find a good chair and to read or at least to skim all of the daily newspapers. Then she stood a while in the woody card catalogue room and looked up authors and titles. According to the list, she checked out and returned on time an average of two novels and one biography per month. The only thing the library lacked, said Parsley, was a tearoom.

When she had something she wanted to look up and the library was closed she used the local mega bookstore as a library. She purchased books only from the Corner Bookstore on Madison and added to her cookbook collection at Kitchen Arts & Letters, where she stood memorizing the ingredients of recipes in a cookbook she couldn't buy. She took out a notebook and pen and started to transcribe it. Owner Nach leaned over her shoulder and said gently, "We *are* a bookstore." They've been BFs ever since. She said the only thing that could improve Kitchen Arts & Letters would be if a bistro or cocktail lounge were attached.

One time she was looking for a recipe for a dish that Thomas Jefferson brought back from Paris, Chartreuse, and she found no less than three books on Jefferson's cooking at Kitchen Arts & Letters—as well as the cookbooks of Colette and Toulouse Lautrec. Jefferson, the inventor of the Lazy Susan, made this with Savoy cabbage. He brought the first seeds for Savoy cabbage to America from Europe and the recipe for Chartreuse from Paris.

Chartreuse is mashed potato bound together by Savoy cabbage, with lemon, butter, mace and cloves. Parsley made it filling an oblong baking dish with individual servings like pigs in a blanket.

Chartreuse à la Thomas Jefferson

Cut out the core and boil a Savoy cabbage for 5 minutes. Plunge in ice water, then drain and cool. Boil and then mash 1 lb. potatoes with cream and butter. Add more butter to a frying pan, and minced carrots, onions and celery, parsley, salt and pepper, lemon zest, and pinches each of cloves and mace. Add vegetables to the mashed potatoes. Blot the cabbage leaves and stuff with potatoes and veg. Place cabbage rolls in a baking dish, dot with butter, and cover with foil. Bake for 20-30 minutes in a 350°F oven (check for doneness before removing, add water and return to the oven if it seems to need that). Before serving, sprinkle with nigella seeds.

𝒯n Parsley's first job in New York—the first of many—
she took her friend's advice and on her job application
made herself Jewish, the better to enjoy more holidays
from work. She never tried that again and felt guilty about
it years later when she ran into the lovely human resources
woman from the old place, who greeted her with "*L'shana
tova!*" Parsley responded, "Same to you!" She celebrated
a couple of holidays on the Jewish calendar, a couple of
holidays on the Christian calendar, and she practiced a
modified version of Ramadan. "I love a fast—especially
a short, fast fast," she said. By and large she went for the
feast days with buffets.

There were few holidays religious or secular that she
found worth ignoring. On St. Pat's Day she wore her green
and yellow T-shirt that says "Kiss Me, I'm Irish" (she's
not) and ate corned beef and cabbage at a bar with Irish
fiddlers. For Shrove Tuesday she prepared *crêpes*. Self-suf-
ficiently, Parsley bought flowers *for herself* on Valentine's
Day if no one else did. She waited until the day after to
buy a more extravagant gift, when roses and chocolates
were marked down.

She frequently brought to work a birthday cake mono-grammed for a co-worker. That sort of cake she made from a package at the last moment, in the dead of night, but she sometimes lied and said she made it from scratch, suggesting it took hours. She ordered a festive bakery cake to use as a centerpiece when she had a dinner party. On her own birthday she sometimes bought a cake, basing her bakery choice on the excellent penmanship of its cake decorator. For a while, the Madison Avenue *pasticceria* Sant Ambroeus had a lot of her business. (How do I know? Parsley saved all of her receipts.)

"My birthday cake does not have to say, 'Happy Birth-day, Parsley.' How childish it would be to insist on that! 'Parsley' will do or my monogram: PZC, for Parsley Zelda Cresswell."

*P*arsley knew Old Quince was not the jealous type or the too-selfish type. Twice married and twice divorced, in spite of his complicated life, Quince liked to have fun—and he picked up the tab. "What can I do for you, my darling?" was practically how he answered the phone. He said, "Making you feel good makes me feel good." He knew how to fight and how to make up, which can be the saving grace of the older boyfriend.

"Oh, Quince. Let's not argue," said Parsley.

"Quarrel over!" he responded, with a warm smile.

Old Quince's mother was a hundred years old. Once a week, on Sunday, he fixed her a delicious meal. Parsley asked, "What did you make?" Quince always replied, "I don't make it, I take it." He brought the Sunday paper and food prepared at his neighborhood restaurant, enough so that his mother had leftovers for a few days. She was losing her mind and often forgot by Monday that he was there on Sunday.

"But all she needs to do is open the refrigerator to be reminded how much her son loves her," said white-haired Quince. "I just hope that someone will bring me Sunday supper when I'm old."

"I will, if I'm around, sweetheart," promised Parsley, with feeling.

Going to dinner at his West Side apartment was a treat. He made ahead just one course, sometimes dessert or an appetizer, and ordered out the rest. "No clean-up!" said Parsley. "You said it!" affirmed Quince.

Thanks to him she learned about the many drugs conveniently produced for the ladies' man to help with "hydraulics," as he put it. Our neighbor Rosemary claimed resolutely to have no familiarity with the little blue pill. Although it was impossible to tell her age, Rosemary was somewhat older than Parsley and achieved a sort of one-upmanship in saying (she was so hot that) all of her boy-friends were younger. Parsley and I found this inspiring.

In respect of his low-salt diet Parsley served Quince unsalted popcorn on Oscar Night. When he visited, she whipped up a nourishing smoothie called a Hippie Hippie Shake, sometimes called You Old Smoothie You. This drink is a scrumptious aid for the digestion of the older boyfriend, who needs fiber.

You Old Smoothie You

Ripe banana or ripe avocado (for fiber)
1 pitted prune (for digestion)
1 T raw chocolate nibs (for his sweet tooth)
½ cup strawberries, raspberries or blueberries
½ cup nonfat plain yogurt

½ cup cranberry or orange juice
½ cup soy or almond milk
½ tsp MSM powder (to curb arthritis)
1 tsp maple syrup (to promote a healthy liver)
1 tsp maca root powder (to boost libido)

With a blender, frozen berries can be used directly from the freezer. An immersion blender works best for smoothies. Or, make a low-tech version: Mash banana and dice prune (and any other fruit used etc.) and add to a hand cocktail shaker with the other ingredients. Shake.

$\mathcal{T}$ he Upper East Side is a bit like Paris—la Rive Droite rather than le Rive Gauche. It's pretty during the winter, under a dusting of snow, shop windows aglow with sparkling lights and glittering merchandise. Tall streetlamps cast shadows of tree branches against townhouses; gold lights and chandeliers flicker inside door lintels. Some trees along Mad Avenue are decorated (some tree huggers say, strangled) with holiday lights. It smells like pine log fires and Chanel No. 5. Neighbors are in even warmer destinations.

Black mink coats come out of storage and sweep down the avenue. Parsley's heaviest winter costume includes furry Himalayan goat boots, a black fox hat, and shearling coat. In this neighborhood one sees more fur coats per capita than anywhere outside of St. Petersburg—one sees even babies in fur and fur capes on dogs.

I feel certain that Parsley will go forth in her Himalayan goat boots, shearling coat, and fox hat once more.

"Here, feel this," Parsley said on a freezing afternoon some years ago, holding open a trench coat lined with supernaturally soft fur. "Chinchilla. I know that it's wrong," she whispered.

During a storm she walked to 92nd St. and Park Avenue to admire snow collecting on the shapes of the Louise Nevelson sculpture, a local landmark. Then, to a little grocery for the ingredients of her weekend soup. Foods of uncertain provenance, not to mention shelf life—pickled jars of anchovies and artichoke hearts—beckon the last-minute Upper East Side shopper. She picked up a can of black beans that looked safe and bought garlic, celery, carrots, Spanish onion, plum tomatoes, parsley, cilantro, and limes from the produce section. She said her heart filled with pride that she was an Upper East Sider at the frozen food section, where she eyed the crustacean selection that included lobster and king crab. She chose a pack of sea scallops.

Scallops and Black Beans

    1 lb. black beans (or 2 cans)
    Olive oil
    4-6 cloves garlic, coarsely chopped
    1 large onion, coarsely chopped
    3 carrots, peeled and cubed

2 stalks celery, peeled and chopped
1 small knob ginger, peeled and chopped
Fresh thyme leaves
Pinches of cinnamon and saffron
Red pepper flakes or Tabasco sauce
Scallops, sea or bay, one pound or less
Juice 1 lemon
1 bay leaf
Kosher salt
Sour cream, parsley, thyme leaves and coriander leaves,
   for garnish
2 limes, quartered
Parsley and coriander, chopped

Pick over beans for pebbles, rinse, and soak the night before in 4 cups of water. (If using canned beans, rinse.) Sauté garlic and onions, carrots and celery in the soup pot, in olive oil. Add ginger, herbs and spices. Add scallops to the pot briefly and remove: add lemon juice and refrigerate until using. (Frozen scallops should defrost fully and be rinsed a couple of times and squeezed dry.)

Add soaked, rinsed beans and 4 cups of fresh water to the pot with vegetables. Bring to a boil and simmer for a couple of hours, stirring. Add bay leaf, parsley and coriander, and salt to taste. Add back the scallops for the last twenty minutes of cooking. Serve garnished with sour cream, parsley, thyme and coriander leaves, and with limes on the side.

*S*he recalled visiting Kyoto in the winter, when hot sweet potatoes were sold on street corners at the end of the day. People returning from work and schoolchildren would buy half a large sweet potato, wrapped in a cone of paper, to peel and eat, without any seasoning or salt. Parsley enjoys a completely plain, baked sweet potato while remembering Japan.

Japanese designers were all Parsley would wear for a time. Yoji Yamamoto's sumo jacket never got so much exposure as it did on Parsley's back. She had a Comme des Garçons padded-shoulder and bustle dress. Some outfit choices have led coworkers to debate whether Parsley Cresswell liked edgy fashion too much. Some days even her makeup pushed the boundaries. She looked especially cute in black eyeliner and a masculine suit.

DRAWING BY JAMES DE LA VEGA

From Japan she also imported the recipe for custard soup called Chawan Mushi (in *Upper East Side Cookbook*, vol. 1) and Oyako Donburi (ditto) and Nasu no den gaku wasu, or Eggplant with Miso.

Eggplant with Miso (Nasu no den gaku wasu)

1 eggplant, sliced
Olive oil to grease the pan
1 T water
2 T miso (unsweetened peanut butter is a substitute)
2 T sugar
1 T ginger, minced
2 cloves garlic, minced

1 T sesame oil
2 T olive oil
2 T rice vinegar
1 T soy sauce or lemon juice
Sesame seeds, pan-roasted

Preheat oven to 400°F. Slice eggplant in half inch slices and place on oiled cooking pan. Dissolve miso in water in a saucepan on the stove. Add sugar, ginger, garlic and other ingredients, except sesame seeds, and simmer until slightly thickened. Brush or spoon the sauce over the eggplant and bake for 20 to 30 minutes, until sauce caramelizes. Sprinkle glazed eggplant slices with sesame seeds before serving.

*O*n the morning of September Eleventh, screening her calls, Parsley saw that Poussiéreuse was on the phone and she picked up. She was drinking her morning tea and reading yesterday's newspaper, economically recovered from the recycling.

"Turn on the television," Poussiéreuse suggested to Parsley. "Which channel?" Parsley asked. "Any one," said Poussiéreuse.

In the following days, she wrote in her diary, "NY deals with a crisis amazingly. An elderly neighbor, eighty years old, worked on the eightieth floor of the last tower standing. When the first plane struck, he began the long descent down the stairwell and kept walking one hundred blocks uptown to his apartment. When he arrived, his neighbor (who had been following his progress by cell phone) greeted him with a plate of cookies warm from the oven. The World Trade Towers have come down. The world is at war. Anybody want a cookie?"

Thereafter, she kept a weatherized denim made-to-order backpack ready to go, with: Chanel lipstick, Maybelline mascara, toothbrush and toothpaste, mint dental floss, a bottle of her signature French scent, sunglasses, Mylar blanket, 6 energy bars, pencils and pens, a fresh Moleskin with important phone numbers and photographs stuck inside, matches, feminine essentials (including close-up mirror and tweezers), paper towels, Xeroxes of her passport and driver's license, 2 surgical masks, 2 lightweight rain ponchos, 3 changes of underwear (black set, white set, blue set), Kleenex, 2 pints of Volvic water, $200 in twenties and tens, Swiss Army knife with corkscrew, mini bird-watching binoculars, transistor radio, digital camera, crosswords, a paperback thriller, flashlight, and an emergency medical kit that includes a miniature bottle of J&B, salt, pepper, mustard, and tea bags.

She showed it off to her Aunt Pistachio, the TWA flight attendant. "You always did pack too much," said her aunt, with a wink. "But now I'd like to be near you during an emergency, to borrow a rain poncho or a spritz of perfume!"

Parsley added a 2 GB thumb drive containing photos, documents and recipes.

*I*n the past she slept late and ate out. She was suspicious of exercise. Rather than join a gym, she blasted music and danced for half an hour. Later on, she took up bird watching. Birding was a reason to be cheerful and a way to stay optimistic. And how could she not bird watch, what with the Barbour utility jacket, Glen plaid vest, Wellington boots, fingerless gloves, Tilley hat, and Pringles of Scotland cashmere scarves? Not to mention, Central Park at her doorstep. She compared notes with restaurateur Céleri Gibson, self-described "ducker", who walked daily twice around the Jackie Kennedy Onassis Reservoir, and kept track of the Buffleheads, Hooded Mergansers, ducklings, and goslings.

In spring and fall Parsley learned to identify Central Park migrants with seasoned birdwatchers, writer Salchicha Caliente and watercolorist Knish Stillman. Warblers ripple down the east coast during fall and winter. They are as small as butterflies and there are a hundred different kinds, identifiable by subtle variations.

Noting Parsley's line of work, Sal and Knish taught her to tell warblers apart according to whether the bird had a pattern of eyeliner, a necklace, or a handkerchief (a white spot on the wing that resembles a handkerchief in a back pocket)—or a crown, a cape, or a hood. Sal said, "Look Parsley, there's a Wilson's warbler. So easy to recognize—he wears a black yarmulke."

The new Parsley rose at 7 to walk in the park before work and brought a peanut butter sandwich, sometimes to share with a bird. She made her best version of oatmeal porridge before setting out on a chilly morning.

Porridge

1 cup water
1 pinch of sea salt
½ cup old-fashioned oats
Fresh ginger, minced
Pinch of cinnamon
Brown sugar
Milk

Boil water, add salt and oatmeal. Stir. Add ginger and cinnamon, cook at a medium simmer till thickened, stirring occasionally. Serve with brown sugar and milk. Optional ingredients: cranberry juice in place of milk, maca root powder or whey (add at the end of the cooking cycle), banana, raisins and toasted walnuts.

G uests can puff away on her terrace. She warned smoking people in the dark to not step on the compost heap.

She accommodated the smokers, yet when she found an old black and white photo of herself with a forbidden cigarette between her index and middle finger, she converted it to digital and photo-shopped out the butt, leaving her fingers in the air in a peace sign. She forgave herself that transgression—back then, people were bombarded by a glamorous image of smoking in movies. When Bran Kempner developed emphysema, Parsley said, "That's it!" Still, she continued to accept guests smoking outdoors, with the "anything goes" atmosphere that she tries to achieve as a hostess.

An autographed Sophia Loren cookbook, *In the Kitchen with Love,* was bookmarked at Sophia's feelings about cigarette smoking at the table. In the great actress's opinion, you must wait until the meal is eaten, that is all. Then, it is permissible for everyone to light up at the table and smoke like chimneys.

Parsley said she believed there should be no cell phones

ever during meals—she wondered how Sophia would feel about cell phones at dinner. Sophia might allow phones at the table only on special occasions—like during a new romance.

She listened to great music while she cooked. In 2006 she was listening to Björk's a cappella "Vespertine." Though she greatly admired Björk's red carpet ball gowns, Parsley was slightly, or more than just slightly, behind everyone else regarding music. "Thank God I discovered Leonard Cohen before I outgrew him."

Many of Parsley's recipes list an interesting provenance. In Morocco with her friend Saffron, she was thrilled to watch the national dish prepared in the kitchen of a Berber woman with tattoos on her face. Parsley's first cookbook, *Setting the Table in a Time of Slender Means* includes a recipe for this unusual savory and sweet pie, but because bistilla is such a good thing to make, here is an alternate recipe. Like her Grandmother Kolache's rule for making pies, make two bistillas while you're at it and freeze one for later.

Bistilla

2 to 3 large chicken breasts
Chicken stock to cover
Cinnamon stick
1 tsp tumeric or a pinch of saffron
1 T minced ginger
3 cloves garlic crushed

1 onion, chopped
1 zucchini, skin and seeds removed and chopped
4 eggs
1 cup slivered almonds, toasted in a pan
1 tsp sugar
1 pinch cinnamon
Phyllo pastry from the grocery
Melted butter to paint on phyllo sheets
Confectioners' sugar
Cinnamon

Boil and reduce to a simmer the chicken stock and seasoning with the (skinned and de-boned) chicken breasts, 20 minutes. Let cool, then shred.

Reduce some of the chicken stock in a pan, and poach the eggs. If eggs are watery, blot excess liquid before mixing it with the shredded chicken.

Toast almonds and cool, then add sugar and cinnamon. Grind the mixture in a food processor, or place in a thick plastic bag and tap with a hammer.

Lay out a newspaper surface to work on. Butter a pie pan and layer with two sheets of refrigerated phyllo pastry that overlap the edges. Layer 6 to 7 phyllo sheets, buttering each with a pastry brush. Spoon a layer of half of the almond-sugar-cinnamon mixture on the bottom of the phyllo-lined pie pan. Drain the chicken-egg mixture, and spoon it over the top of the almond layer. Add another almond layer, before folding in the phyllo, adding folded layers on top and tucking it around the sides before baking for around 20 minutes at 400°F, or until golden brown. Decorate with a dusting of confectioners' sugar and cinnamon.

*P*arsley struggled to keep a small nest egg intact, at the same time, she started to use the good china for every day. The financial crisis caused her to fall back on artistic talents. She was capable of giving herself a professional looking manicure, though she preferred nail salons because of their congeniality. She started to color her own hair. Poussiéreuse showed her how, "Saving me about a million dollars."

"What more could we want, Franny? This is the good life—recession or no recession."

In some respects I had to agree. We lived in a part of town that looked like Paris in springtime, even in winter, but losing one's job pulls the rug out from under one. My job was eliminated in a sweeping cutback.

So it was that I had the leisure to study Parsley's food files when she went away. Becoming her unofficial biographer meant I did a stealth audit of her situation. It proved to be the most rewarding work I have ever done as a C.P.A., because I found that while she didn't have much, she was not broke—in fact, Parsley energetically kept the wolf from the door. She rose above the downward spiral.

She remade her résumé, removing the date of her birth, which was in any case an underestimation. Admirably, she tried out new work and reinvented herself. This fossilized apartment, the ornate shell she left behind, became where I went to feel that all's well in the world.

PC was nothing if not versatile. In one of her many jobs, briefly, she freelanced as a dominatrix. Was it a sound business model? I doubt it. I frankly wondered how she ever did it, but she assured me that I too could be dominatrix, with the right styling, should I ever get tired of being a bookkeeper!

In late 2008, Parsley Cresswell was arrested following an unfortunate accident in which her client, a 76 year old hedge fund manager, suffered a heart attack while he was with her, tied face-down to the hotel bed (at his request) with grosgrain ribbons, in his preferred form of physical therapy. She herself placed the 911 call and fretfully waited for medics to arrive and revive him, only to be charged with involuntary manslaughter.

About that line of work, Parsley said, a little defensively, "Well, you can imagine how much I would love the clothes, the accessories! C'mon!"

*H*er favorite part of the runway show was the bridal gown modeled last, before the finale. She'd been a bridesmaid too many times, and a bride just once, not to be a sucker for weddings.

Parsley went to City Hall for the nuptials of a friend and threw rice and cried (in waterproof mascara), all innocent of the fact that it was a green card wedding.

Two Unusual Wedding Cakes For the New York wedding reception of Angelica and Javier Frappuccino, who married in Las Vegas, she made an easily transportable (before assembly), two-foot tower of cereal-marshmallow bars, drizzled with melted, semi-sweet chocolate, white chocolate curls, and marshmallow Peeps. Rice Krispies squares were involved, using the recipe on the package of Rice Krispies cereal, 2 or 3 batches, and also cubed **Popcorn Cake**: 1 cup butter and 1 cup vegetable oil, 3 quarts popcorn, 1 can mixed nuts, 1 lb. cup-up marshmallows, 1 lb. semisweet chocolate chips. Melt together butter, oil, and marshmallows, stirring. Add popcorn, nuts and chocolate chips. With buttered fingers, press into buttered pans and allow to cool, before cutting with a sharp knife and packing to travel or assembling on the spot.

When lesbian friends, Clementine and Ginger, got married at the dude ranch in Door County, Parsley made for their reception a five-tiered **Wisconsin Cheese Wheel Wedding Cake**, decorated with seasonal fruits and flowers and two little brides on top.

PHOTOGRAPH BY PARSLEY CRESSWELL

EPILOGUE

*A*fter I found the steamer trunk with her recipe archive I knew Parsley that much better. She had a modest liquid investment portfolio, paid down debts, and was never delinquent on taxes. Far from it! "I love to pay my taxes," she has said. This was true: Some years she overpaid the IRS. She was a model citizen! I was proud to know her.

We talked from the prison phone, and I was always sharply aware as she spoke, *sotto voce*, that she felt distanced from the uptown girl she once was. I was her dedicated listener. I would be lying if I didn't add that I sometimes felt she was whining.

"I'm always in the mood for a fine whine," as Parsley says.

She encourages one to let it all hang out, a skill that doubtless makes her popular in prison. It was rough there, no doubt, yet her prison cell was actually four times the size of the cubicle I had worked in at a Fortune 500 company. It wasn't summer camp, and though she was never again as chipper as she once was, Parsley could still find good things to say about her situation. It gave one hope.

The only time I noticed her spirit waver was during the call in which she said she lost a lot in a bad investment, through a tip from neighbors, Plum and Herb de Provence.

"My heart goes out to you," I said, with genuine sympathy. Only an accountant can be so emotional, so gullible, around numbers.

"It's only money," she said, with admirable nonchalance. "As Bobby would say, 'Don't think twice. It's alright'."

Parsley left diverse notes in a folder called *Notes to Self.* "Eat local honey during allergy season." "Mercury retrograde is ideal for weeding out drawers and closets and editing photos." "An Apple a Day: a banana a day, a carrot a day, and an apple a day, <u>in that order</u>." A more puzzling entry, on corsets, went, "When you are being laced into a whalebone corset, do NOT suck in your stomach."

"Vegan: try not to give up cheese. Why deny yourself?" Her words of warning are few and far between: "Don't watch scary movies except at matinees. Hug your teddy bear to go to sleep. Exercise caution during a high tide—avoid salt and cheese. Pizza on the night of the full moon will cause a nightmare or, at least, a scary moment when you step on the scale the morning after. Be your own chef in the evening and you escape the dark thoughts that spring up between one and four a.m. Eat well, and you will sleep on, have a fantastic dream, and wake up refreshed, looking forward to your newspaper and *petit déjeuner.* Now go to bed."

On popcorn: "Use as garnish on soup and salad. Serve as a side dish." A note on going organic: "Potatoes, onions, carrots: Root vegetables need to be organic. Milk: organic and growth hormone-free. Eggs: free range. Buy organic tomatoes, peppers, zucchini, and eggplant as soon as you can afford to." (As usual, her writing strikes a hopeful note!)

"When the temperature soars, make **Blueberry Granita**: blend on high 1 cup frozen blueberries and ½ cup yogurt. Eat with a spoon in a cool, darkened room."

There were many more tips. She had a recipe for reversing bad juju and one for shucking off guilt. I came to think of her as a sorcerer devising magic potions, like her fabled matzo ball soup—through experimentation she determined that the healthiest soup was not chicken but matzo ball. She wasn't the food snob I took her for. Fresh parsley, flat or curly—it's all the same to her. She didn't care about the virginity of her olive oil.

It seemed a touchstone in Parsley's culinary experience that in 1994 she attended a luncheon at Julia Child's house in Cambridge, Mass., with her friend Marjolaine, who had studied at Le Cordon Bleu in Paris. When Parsley returned from this historic trip, she tacked up on the wall a picture of herself and Marjolaine with Julia. Then she repainted her entire apartment green, in homage to Julia's penchant for that color. "Julia had a pale green kitchen, a moss green dining room, hunter green in the living room and a grass green downstairs bathroom."

DRAWING BY PHOEBE DINGWALL.

Here I part company with PC, who makes the Sign of the Cross whenever she hears the name Julia Child. For a while I attempted more in my own kitchenette, usually aided by that too difficult cookbook, *Mastering the Art of French Cooking*. Julia Child: the bane of my cooking existence. (Parsley promised I'd like her if I watch "The French Chef," her TV series.)

One of the last articles she filed before she went to jail was titled *The Nun Study*. "Completed in 2001, with over 600 nuns at convents across Wisconsin and Minnesota, the so-called nun study shows that the happier we can manage to be, the longer we shall live. The sisters were observed over several decades. The positive, talkative nuns escaped the ravages of age." This doesn't sound like someone capable of manslaughter.

Another draft she left, complete with blue-pencil scribbles, was an article for *O Magazine* on finger food, floral arrangement, and party planning. She appeared to be working on it at the last minute. It begins: "Everyone can rely on you to provide good food and stimulating conversation. Create a festive mood with Brazilian music or jazz and tall flower arrangements around the room rather than a centerpiece. Mix stems of dark basil and mint with your flowers, and pheasant feathers to give it that McQ touch. Instruct people to park their inhibitions, along with shoes, at the door. Probably surprise parties are to be avoided for any birthday past the fiftieth as liable to cause a cardiac event. Have a 'come as you are' dress code, however invite everyone well ahead of time so they can work out their best outfit—particularly the guest of honor. Appoint a guest of honor."

That was the Parsley I knew. Unable to do the things she loved, such as write articles about bold-faced names, I wondered what she was doing.

"Not to worry, Fran. There's a lot to do! I'm collecting recipes from all my new friends." Parsley said that she was meeting more women who cooked and shared their recipes *there* than she ever did on the Upper East Side, in "our skinny-bitch neighborhood."

Parsley was on her way to being sprung. We signed up a dream team: Porto Bello and Wheat Read. I peeled off hundred dollar bills to pay them from the box of what we called "salad."

If anyone should know that she was innocent, it is I, her asset manager. When digging through her recipes I found her Chase Manhattan bank statements last of all, with small amounts in checking and savings. I knew that she lived frugally.

If she had had even a bit more cash, Parsley Cresswell would have gone out to restaurants more often, not to mention cook with ingredients other than onions, mushrooms, lentils, rice and chicken. For she was *even more frugal* in the months that led up to her arrest. If she knew then that a substantial amount of cash was coming her way she would not have restricted herself so. I would never have bothered to look for this needle in the haystack were it not for the gift from a fan, sent in a Fresh Direct package.

Parsley checked to see that her knives were sharpened—she was fanatical about sharp knives, calling from the echoing corridor to make sure that I've taken them to the man inside the little cart.

"What I wouldn't give for a good sharp file now," she said. "Any more produce from Fresh Direct?"

"No," I said. "But that last one nearly made a vegan out of me."

"I hear you," she said.

She mentioned she was inked and bragged, "I got the same tattoo that Martha got!"

She said she gave up everything but her persistent sweet tooth. Ah, so that accounted for her slight weight gain.

"Fortunately, vegetarians can still eat sweets," she said.

"You're a vegetarian now?" I couldn't be more shocked.

She said she had a dream in prison about the future, *à la* Eric Blair and *1984*, in which we eat only grains, fruits and vegetables (and eggs and cheese, of course), but no meat and no fish. It's an abstemious vision, but not quite hair shirt, because it allows dairy products.

"I might join the vegans—it's good for the figure, after all—were it not for my love of cheese." She waxed nostalgic about the tomatoes and the sweet corn she was missing.

The call gave me the chance to try to answer the burning question—whether indeed she knows "Bob", Bob Dylan. Even though I was a close ally, looking after her financial house, not to mention her cantankerous bird, Gougère, I still felt shy about asking.

Blasé, she sighed. "Yes, of course. I gave him the lyric in *Lay, Lady, Lay,* 'You can have your cake and eat it, too.' I thought you knew that."

Voila!

It's taking longer than I thought to tell Parsley's story. For the life of Lyndon B. Johnson, Robert Caro needed three volumes. Another is required for Parsley Cresswell. Here we are on Volume 2, and she hasn't started what will surely be the best chapter in her life so far. The next *UES Cookbook*, I shall step aside. Parsley will tell her own story of recipe collecting around the world and inside the big house, from her fellow inmates who, after all, cook more than people do on the Upper East Side.

Expect an *amuse bouche* and a tempting *entrée*. Park your "inhibitions, along with shoes, at the door." Parsley is a gracious hostess and always finds the right thing to say. I'll never forget the time I told her I was out of sorts, overworked, sleep-deprived, and she replied: "Take two fresh eggs, whisk, add chopped spinach and herbs, grated cheese, a dash of Tabasco, fry gently, and eat with whole wheat toast."

Fran Smith C.P.A.

DRAWING BY JENNIFER OLLE

APPENDIX

Readers complained about the crab cake recipe that used canned crab in volume one of *The Upper East Side Cookbook, Setting the Table in a Time of Slender Means*. Of course, Parsley agrees that it is inexcusable to use canned crab. This better version of crab cake has fresh crab and avoids mayonnaise. Hold the mayo! Especially when the weather is warm. Parsley makes this dish whenever she feels crabby.

Crab Cakes

  1 lb. crab meat
  1 tsp Dijon mustard
  Pimento, diced
  2 T Old Bay seasoning
  Soft bread crumbs for binding, from 2 slices of bread
  ¼ cup chopped parsley
  More chopped parsley for garnish
  Lemon wedges
  Olive or vegetable oil

After forming small patties, the size of hockey pucks, dredge them in bread crumbs. Refrigerate for 15 minutes to allow firming up. Fry in half-inch deep oil on medium heat. Garnish with chopped parsley and lemon wedges.

INDEX

Parsley's creator, Linda Olle, was born on a dairy farm in Racine, Wisconsin. She has lived and worked on the Upper East Side of New York for thirty years and absorbed its secrets. Most nights she falls asleep with a cookbook in her hands, often wishing that cookbooks had plots. *Main Course* is the second in the series that began with the 2009 *The Upper East Side Cookbook: Setting the Table in a Time of Slender Means.*

DEDICATION

For artistic contribution, I dedicate this to Leeta Taylor,
Jane Freeman, Joan Leonard, Mary Leonard, Roz Tornatore,
Howard Stillman, Anita Stillman, Dusty Mortimer-Maddox,
Anne E. Putnam, Peter Canby, Catherine Stock, Abbe Bates,
Phoebe Dingwall, Garrison Keillor, Jensen Wheeler Wolfe,
Becca Pulliam, Lauri Gibson, Vivek Bandhu, Roberta White,
Susan Lewis, Adele De Cruz, Victor Albrow, Diane Torr, Dean
Leslie, Mary Flannery, Amy Flannery, Zora O'Neill, Brian
Lehrer, Tenaya Darlington, Gina James, Silvano Nova, Craig
Seligman, Mary Davis Haling, Al Holter, Joanna Fortnam,
Sheila Dillon, Kath Davies, OBE, Rose Pipes, Kate Babyak,
Sumana Raychaudhuri, Ellen Pearlstein, and Steven Vecchio.

Visit Parsley Cresswell on Facebook for instant friendship.

Made in the USA
Charleston, SC
21 November 2011